EVA WOLF

A shatter in the dark

First edition

Narration by Sarah rozzier

This book was professionally typeset on Reedsy.
Find out more at reedsy.com

Contents

This isn't a good story

The first thing you should know about me is I am a whore!

My life was like a scale being tipped back and forth until one side finally outweighed the other, a trigger, a moment of impulsivity, a window of opportunity that disrupted the precarious balance that allowed me to survive.

That back and forth was exhausting, and it muddled my judgment.

I was at this point completely exhausted from life itself, with no option but to seek some help, I really couldn't do this on my own. The darkness was with me nearly every time I woke up. I felt like a grime was covering me. I felt like I was trapped in a contaminated body that no amount of washing would clean. Whenever I thought about him I felt manic and itchy and couldn't concentrate on anything else. It manifested itself in purging or self-harming for days at a time or sleeping for sixteen hours straight or drinking binges that lead to promiscuous sex. I was exhausted from feeling like this every hour of every day.

Three to four nights a week I had nightmares about him. It made me want to avoid sleep and I was constantly tired because sleeping with what feels like hours of nightmares is not restful. I woke up sweaty, distressed, and angry. I was reminded every morning of what was done to me and its control over my life.

Alcohol was something that let me escape the darkness. It would always find me later, though, and it was always angry that I managed to escape and it made me pay. Many of the irresponsible things I did were the result of the darkness. Obviously, I'm responsible for every decision and action, including this one, but there are reasons why things happen the way they do.

Alcohol and other drugs provided a way to ignore the realities of my situation. It was easy to spend the night drinking and forget that I had no future to look forward to. I never liked what alcohol did to me, but it was better than facing my existence honestly. The darkness will always be with me.

And so there I was standing outside the psychiatrist's office not exactly sure what would lie ahead, but knowing there was no going back. I needed to be free from my past, and the trauma which had been paralyzing me for over twenty years.

After all, I had tried everything else, so it was now or never.

I gave the door three knocks and waited. My heart was beating so fast, my palms sweaty, my throat dry. After a short while, the door opened to a lady dressed in casual clothes her hair tied into a ponytail. She had an aura around her that immediately made me feel at ease ."You must be Eva" she introduced herself."I'm Claire"

I smiled a nervous smile and followed her into a room. It

was bare with just two armchairs facing each other, a small table and a painting on the wall and a clock on the other.

I sat down wondering what this would entail hoping she would not ask me what I really knew I was there to talk about. We both sat for a moment in silence looking at each other until finally, Claire interluded."What is it that has brought you here today Eva?" her voice soft and calming. I shuffled uncomfortably in my chair "i i i"i stuttered.Usually I have no problem in talking just ask my friends,but in these situations or high levels of stress and anxiety my childhood stutter reappears.

"Take your time," Claire said comfortingly.

"I'm just a broken, miserable shell of a human being. Being abused has defined me as a person and shaped me as a human being and it has made me the monster I am and there's nothing I can do to escape it. I don't know any other existence. I don't know what life feels like where I'm apart from any of this. I actively despise the person I am. I just feel fundamentally broken, almost non-human. I feel like an animal that woke up one day in a human body, trying to make sense of a foreign world, living among creatures it doesn't understand and can't connect with." I blurted out hardly stopping to take a breath.

"That sounds very difficult for you," Claire said again with a calming voice that seemed to understand my pain.

"Well I suppose I should just start near the beginning, I mean if I tell you my story which isn't a good story, and then go from there," I said nervously thinking to myself that I had never told anyone any of this in my life. Claire nods at me to continue, and so this is my story the best way I know how to tell it.

Why don't you love me

From the start, I wasn't the daughter my mother wanted and she wasn't the mother I needed. The second-born child to Evelyn Wolf, I was an alien creature with an independent spirit and overwhelming needs.

I was "naughty" – I stayed awake, crying inconsolably for her return. In later years, kneeling on the carpet by the side of my bed, I would have to repeat: "God bless Daddy, God bless Mummy. If I have been a bad girl today, make me a good girl tomorrow." Fat chance – I had the devil in me.

"The problem with you, Eva" she would say, "is that you always want to be the centre of attention."

I lost my mother when I finally found my voice and contradicted her. This wasn't in her motherly plan.

"I don't know where you get it from," she would remark. "You must be adopted or dropped on the wrong doorstep."

And this from a woman who had been fostering since I was two! Far too busy helping others to spend any time with me. I was always at the bottom of a very long list of other things she needed to do first.

My status as a public embarrassment was sealed. Especially when I grabbed the front page of the Gazette. "What will the neighbours say, Eva?"

It's difficult to love a cuckoo – I understand that now. When children reflect on their parents' aims, aspirations, and personal traits, there's a warm, fuzzy glow all around.

Discovering, when I was 13, that I had a sex life was the last straw for my mother. "You'll get pregnant" she exclaimed as she moulded pastry round a pie dish.

Why did I have to be such a changeling? Why couldn't I stay still, be normal and behave myself? My indefatigable energy made me uncontrollable.

But still, I wanted to please my mother, to hear her tell me she loved me. I wanted her to say that she was proud of what I'd achieved, of my children – her grandchildren – of my long,

5

happy marriage and beautiful home. I wanted acceptance. Whatever I chose, whatever path I took, it was always the wrong one for my mother.

I had gone off the rails after my father announced he was leaving two weeks before Christmas. Already a troubled teen with the body of a twenty-year-old and a defiant attitude it was no wonder I was going to cross his path. After that fateful night where he took more than my virginity, I was unable to get through a day without thinking about him, without longing to see him again but the constant following me around or waiting at the school gates for me was becoming incessant, and although I wanted it to stop I also wanted to be with him. I knew it was wrong but my mind had already been changed so that I couldn't think for myself.

You might be thinking, "who lets their 13-year-old daughter go off with a 26-year-old?"

Well, my mother couldn't care less where I was. It's not on purpose she just wasn't paying attention to anything.

Sometimes he would pick me up from a local park that was away from the house so my mother would not get suspicious of me getting into a random car. He would drive fast with loud music blasting out, the windows open, and my hair blowing in my face. We had a laugh and got on really well. He said he really liked me and that I was really different from the other girls he knew. We would chat, talk about how much I hated life, and when we got to the flat we would just chill listening to music, and having sex.

Steve took me to really cool parties with all his friends. They were all really nice and I had a really good time. Steve said I was mature for my age. He encouraged me to drink he said it would make me have a better time.

My mother used to go mad when I didn't come home until the morning after but I didn't care, I wanted to spend all my time with Steve. Sometimes I'd stay at Steve's for a few days. We'd just hang around his flat. Mum even reported me missing to the police but I thought she was just over-reacting.

I was constantly truanting from school to be with him, and the school called meetings with my mother and my father but nothing serious ever came of it.

Steve would call my home phone and let it ring three times to let me know it was him. I would then have to run to the phonebox at the end of the road and wait for it to ring. Then he would tell me where and when I would be picked up. If it was late at night I would climb out of my bedroom window leaving it slightly ajar in case I needed to sneak back in. Then onto the flat roof of the porch and then down the fence.

Steve would be waiting on the other side of the park for me.

Steve who was more than twice my age expected me to return sexual favors for the gifts and kindness he gave me. Usually, I was too drunk or too high to know exactly what was going on around me. Reality often drifted away and I would wake up in a bed in my underwear, my clothes on the floor. Sometimes his friend would be at the flat too and sometimes there were more friends there. His friends would have sex with me, and I would just lie there. I had no feelings. They would get up after and go to the bathroom to clean up leaving me with the smell I hated, the smell of sex. I would stand in the shower for ages scrubbing myself trying to get rid of it, but it was in my nose and stayed with me for a long time afterward. They were all older and all intimidating. Some of the men took hard drugs such as cocaine and heroin. I was on my own and life was just going by in slow motion.

Today I became a prostitute. Now I no longer live a conventional life.

Life became a living nightmare. A nightmare which I could not wake up from. What began as me looking for freedom from my home life turned into four years of abuse, exploitation, and violence. If I could, I would have just walked away.

Then, I met my soul mate: cocaine. This drug was the epitome of perfection to me. I could forget what was being done to me, I could work without stopping, and lose weight—all at the same time. I loved the feeling I got on day one and chased it for the next 3 years because any beatings were quickly hidden by another few white lines.I was trapped in a cycle of love and abuse

But Without him the pain was unbearable I couldn't eat or sleep, sometimes it felt like I couldn't breathe and so I was with him more often than not.

This particular day was like no other but I had missed so much of school and the concerns around my welfare amongst the teachers and other authorities were becoming harder to dodge and so I just had to go to school at least to put them off the scent and I would tell him later that he had to stay away from the school.

I was walking to school and looked around to see his car parked by the side of the road. I thought to myself how did he know I would walk this way? why is he waiting for me? I'm still supposed to be in school. He gets out and starts walking towards me and I start to run as fast as I can. I know it seems a bit over the top but last time he beat me so badly and broke my arm and I had to tell my mother I did it during sports.

I ran towards the park trying to avoid people's confused stares, but I didn't get very far before Steve had caught me. He pulled my hair and slapped me as hard as he could so I fell to the ground, he's still holding me by the hair so I scratch his hand which releases his grip on me. I try to get up and run but he punches me hard in the back of the head and I fall to the ground.

"I'm sorry" I whisper trying to get some sympathy from him
He turns me around and stares fiercely into my scared eyes "you will be"
He takes me by the hand and pulls me to my feet his grip on me is strong and marches me back through the park towards his parked car. Just before we reach the car one of my classmates shouts are you ok? and before I could speak he tells her that he was chasing after me because I said I was going to kill myself and that I fell down the hill when I saw him but everything's ok now.

Steve forces me into the back of the car I try to fight, but of course, I lost.

As soon as we arrive outside his flat he drags me inside pushes me to the floor and locks the door, I get up only for my face to be pushed into the floor again. Tears stream down my face as I start to cry. Bending down to my level he forcefully grabs my chin so that I look at him.

"Now will you try and run from me again!" he asks
I whisper a "no" back whilst shaking my head
He stands me up grabbing my hair and punches me in the face. "Huh? baby, I didn't hear you" his voice gruff.
"no" I squeal a little louder the pain of being held up by my hair.

Steve sniggers at the sound of pain that leaves my lips
"What was that," he says slapping me to the floor again. I was sobbing so loud I couldn't hear what he said so he hits me

again.

"NO ILL NEVER RUN FROM YOU AGAIN IM SORRY" I scream as loud as I can praying to God he will stop.

But the onslaught continues with him kicking me in the stomach and ribs ,i lose count of the blows to the side of my head i think i'm concussed.

He takes me to his room throws me on the bed locks the door and leaves. I lay there in the silence wondering how long i will be locked in for.At least its not the cellar ,and i have a bathroom.I huddle up in the covers waiting listening to the ticking clock thats ticking loudly in my head.Time seems to stand still until i drift off to sleep.When i wake its daylight,i think its late afternoon though as i can here children playing outside.Soon I get enough strength to take myself into the bathroom and look at myself my side is so painful i wince as i lift my school shirt up to see the bruises,i'm black and blue it looks bad so i cover up again not wanting to look at myself. I head back to his room and open my backpack and take out my diary. Tears descend as I begin to jot down my sorrow.

what is love? I do not understand it. they say love hurts... .but I didn't know it would hurt this bad. I don't think he really loves me? can't he see I already go through enough as it is? I don't need to feel any more stupid, rejected, or useless than I already feel. can't he see me crying and broken? Don't you see you're hurting me?

sometimes I know it's my fault. I just don't listen or I have to lie

I know I should leave. I should get help

But I need him, I want him. God help me because I love him.

It's getting late again and i I had fallen asleep. I bang on the door shouting to Steve to let me out, but theres no reply. He

10

would have to let me leave at some point so I could go home. Eventually, he unlocks the door and sits beside me. He thinks I'm pathetic. He says he doesn't want to hurt me but I make it impossible sometimes that it will all be fine if I just listen to him, if I just stay and never go home.

He can see the shocked look on my face and reassures me that it will be okay, that he just wants to be with me always that my family doesn't want me anyway and that he can look after me. I nod in agreement as he caresses my face. I get up and walk towards the door he steps in front of me each step forward he takes pushes me back until I'm pinned against the wall. I start thinking the worst, but instead, it's the complete opposite."I'm sorry, I didn't want to hurt you, I love you, you still love me don't you?"

"Yes of course i love you"i whisper

Steve takes me by the hand and we both sit on the end of the bed.

I tell myself he's manipulating me that I will not fall for it. I tell myself that it's my fault that I'm difficult and make him angry. I say I'm sorry too he kisses me hard on the lips his hand pushing up my school skirt, ripping my knickers off with one hand he undoes his jeans releasing his erection lifting my leg up he thrusts into me fucking me until he comes.

"I own you" he announces, triumphantly

He slumps on the bed satisfied, at last, and turns over and goes to sleep.

I was so scared I didn't dare move. Soon he was snoring loudly. I tried to very gently roll away from him so i didn't have to smell that smell, though I realised it was me I hadn't washed in two days or changed underwear.

I lay there in the darkness wounded, throbbing in pain. My

mind in turmoil.I tried to separate my mind from my body, to distance my thoughts, but I was in so much pain.I was in hell, How had I got here?

I thought about what I could do to get away from him, but my brain was shaken and confused.I needed to think.I thought about slipping past him but no he would surely wake.

Every inch of my body was battered, assaulted by sharp pangs of pain as if I had been stabbed.I had nothing left, my resistance was spent....That night I wet the bed for the first time since I was a toddler,I lay there in the wet cold sheets all night wallowing in misery.

Perhaps he would leave me alone now for a few days at least as he had had his fun with me. It was the only thing I could hope for right now. As I lay there in the darkness, my body on fire my ears full of white noise, listening to his snoring. I thought if only I could just smother him now with my pillow,but I knew that he was much to strong for me.

I couldn't leave he had already infected my young mind and so I stayed.

Going out to meet and have sex with men became normal for me. Every time I thought about fighting back, the threats of him hurting me would stop me. I was reluctant to get help, even though I knew it was wrong.

Time out by myself was a rare thing but occasionally I would be allowed to the shop and these few moments of freedom were what I lived for.

I slowly slipped on my red converse ready to go to the corner shop. As I grabbed my coat from the hook in the hallway, I hear his voice.

"And where do you think you're going?"Steve snorted

"Oh I was just going to go to the shop to get some cigarettes and a bar of chocolate " my voice muffled

We both just stood there whilst he quietly pondered.

Steve rolls his eyes and sighs heavily "ok but you better be back in 30 minutes or you'll regret it!" his voice low and angry

"Crystal…." I reply back trying not to sound annoyed. I take a deep breath and silently give Steve a little wave as I walk out shutting the door behind me. I press play on my Walkman and turn the volume up to max Ah-ha cry wolf comes on as I stroll along taking in the fresh air, the trees lining the road. I try not to dawdle as I know I'm on a time limit. After a few minutes, I arrived at the shop and pushed on the door but it won't open, I try to push again then I see the big blue writing saying pull to open. God, I must look like a total idiot. I feel so awkward but join the queue and gaze at the chocolate I decide on a mars bar. The girl behind the counter is happy and smiles as she asks me what id like, and I wish I could be that happy. Or maybe she's faking it and hiding her pain like me.

I'm trying not to let these dark thoughts invade my head. I take off my headphones "I'll have twenty Marlborough red please and a lighter," I said to her quickly placing the chocolate on the counter whilst fumbling in my pocket for a fiver. She rings it up on the till and passes me the pack of cigarettes. I turn swiftly and exit the shop. Stepping outside and I rip the cellophane from the pack and take out a cigarette lighting it with the lighter I just brought. The flame flickers as I take a drag. I start to head back towards our flat when a guy stops me he looks disheveled probably homeless. I sigh as he approaches me asking if I have a spare cigarette. I reach into my pocket and take out the newly opened pack and offer him a cigarette. "Please take two," I said feeling sorry for him.

"Thank you" he mumbled back.

I smiled at him and carried on smoking as I walked along the path. Halfway there's a bench and a small green so I stopped to enjoy the fresh air and listen to my Walkman, Madonna, Erasure, Bon Jovi and Kim Wilde play and I'm losing myself in their songs. Being outside by myself was a rarety so I wanted to enjoy it for as long as possible. I stamp out the burning end of my cigarette and light another. then I realize that I was supposed to be back in 30 minutes. I'm panicking thinking I'm going to be late, so I start to run and am out of breath when I get to the flat. I quietly and slowly open the flat door and go in.

Steve is standing there his arms crossed breathing heavy and looking me up and down.

"You're late" he hisses at me I gulp and start to tremble. "How late?" I answer my voice shaky.

"two minutes!" he yells right in my face. I can see his clenched fist as I look down and bite my lip trying not to show fear or emotion.

"I'm sorry" my face is already getting red and puffy. He's continuing to yell at me.

"What happens when you're late?" he screams in my ear nearly deafening me. I shook my head and before I knew it I felt a hard punch in my side. The tears start to fall down my cheeks. Steve walks off into the kitchen and slams his fists down on the sideboard making me jump.

I walk off to the bathroom and lock the door sliding to my knees and crying uncontrollably. The tears make my eyes red and puffy as I try to wipe them away. I feel so broken. Someone save me from this hell.

The next day I wake up early Steve is still sleeping, I slowly tiptoe to the bedroom door hoping not to wake him I slip through the door and peek through the gap he is still asleep. I can shower in peace. After a hot shower, I dress and make coffee. I sit up on the windowsill with the steaming hot cup and smoke a cigarette out of the kitchen window. These things I do enjoy and would never have been able to do when I lived at home.

No, I have everything I need right here, I can't go back now, it's tough sometimes but it will get better if I just try harder, I tell myself.

I finish my cigarette just as Steve walks into the kitchen. "You're up early, I was hoping you would still be asleep so I could wake you" his words playful. He walks towards where I'm perched and takes hold of my ankles pulling me to him. We start to kiss as he fondles my breasts. "God you get me so hard in the morning" his voice deep and husky in my ear. His words immediately excite me and I feel myself getting wet, his hands already in my knickers toying with my tight bud. I cannot contain my pleasure and moans escape my lips. "Show me how hard you are," I say.

Removing his pyjama bottoms he reveals his huge hard cock throbbing to attention, just the sight makes me so horny I want him in me to feel his thickness. I remove my bottoms and knickers and sit on the countertop my legs open in anticipation. He pulls me so I'm perching right on the edge my wet lips there for all to see and thrusts himself into me. I squeal with delight as his cock stretches me and fills me. I'm on the edge of orgasm already and he knows how much I want him. As he thrusts deeper quicker and harder into me I feel myself losing all thoughts of the day before, I'm consumed by my sexual desire for him and nothing else matters. I couldn't get enough of him. I was tired and sore but I didn't care. I didn't want

15

to sleep. I wanted the ache. I wanted him in me, all the time. His weight on top of me. I wanted to squeeze him in further and further. I wanted to watch his face. I wanted his sweat to drop onto me. My orgasm can be probably be heard by half the street. I allow myself to vocalize my pleasure instead of masturbating in quiet at my childhood home. He has liberated me and I scream loud and proud.

I never want to go back home, besides I would never fit back in. I have been shown how beautiful my body is, how to be confident in my nakedness, I know how to give myself the ultimate pleasure and how to take that pleasure too. I'm like a pink rose opening her petals for all the world to see. My sexual desires seem to be at their peak and then I find myself at a new height and I cannot get enough. After being shut down by my mother's oppressive Christian views I'm so hungry for pleasure that I feel I would die without it.

We break for a while to recover and then he's hard again the head of his penis tingling unbearably; it was hot and swollen, a drop forming at the tip and I take him in my mouth each suck of his flesh heightening my arousal I want him everywhere to touch every inch of my body and soul to fuck me in every hole to chastize me to spank me with his bare hand until I collapse from exhaustion. Steve is well aware of my neediness and takes me to the edge and back again until I cry out for my orgasm. Now I need rest for my time with him is coming to an end and I will return to the terraced house to sleep, eat and work until he wants me again and I pray he won't stay away too long.

Broken from a young age

In my hands was my baby the size and shape of a small water balloon and the deepest shade of scarlet. Holding my bundle, carefully swaddled in toilet paper, I fought back the tears that were choking me as I flushed my unborn baby down the toilet

The fear and pain I had just endured washed away but imprinted on my soul

I stood there my legs trembling, blood still streaming down my thighs, my heart racing, he would be home soon.

"Maybe he will comfort me if I tell him?"I tell myself inside my head "Don't be stupid he will be so angry, I don't want that" I stood in the shower letting the water wash away my shame, my body aching from the contractions my legs weak. Time stood still my head a whirlwind of hazing thoughts the sound of the water splashing the tiles my focus.

The trauma does not just lie in the horrors of watching dreams and children die; the trauma comes in the questions we face and the decisions we must make about the most difficult moments a person will endure.

This was the only decision/choice I had but I was not prepared for the pain or loss that would come from my desperate attempt with a wire coat hanger and copious amounts of alcohol. Harry had helped me when the pain was too unbearable for me to continue by myself.

I wrapped myself in a warm towel hoping it would offer my body some comfort and sat on the bathroom floor for what seemed like hours, I was not sure but I had begun to feel cold.

The sound of the door opening and footsteps startled me."Eva" he called

"I'm in the bathroom" I replied trying to control the wobble in my voice

"You should be ready by now, I have a client booked!" his voice was abrasive

"But I can't" the words had left my mouth before I had realized what I had said.

The door was flung open he stood there his face hard and angry, he grabbed me forcefully by the wrist, dragging me along "all you do is whine!" his voice is angry his nostrils flaring his eyes wild with aggression.

Steve opens the wardrobe door and throws a black dress on the bed, then rummages through my underwear drawer and pulls out a blue set." Here now get the fuck ready" and he turned abruptly and headed towards the kitchen.

I sob the hot tears rolling down my cheeks "I can't I'm sorry I'm not well" my throat closing up as I speak the words. I felt as if I was going to throw up.

Steve charges at me his eyes dark and wide with rage his hands immediately round my throat squeezing me till I struggle to breathe. We struggle as I flay my arms out to try

18

and push him off me, legs kicking so hard in the fight for my life I bang my head on the corner of something dazing myself for a moment, my eyes wide with fear and helplessness. He's on top of me looking me straight in the eye

"Please stop" I squeak hardly being able to muster the words. Steve removes his hands from my throat and backs away, hesitating for a moment, my eyes wide with fear and helplessness I gather the towel back around me, as I do he notices a trickle of blood running down my thigh. his face is empty, a tear rolls down my cheek, I crouch in the corner in apprehension of the beating that I knew would come.

Grabbing me by the hair this time pulling me towards the bathroom, in silence he rips away the towel and pushes me into the shower.

"do you think you can just run your pretty mouth off at me whenever you want?!"I mumble a "no" back my voice barely a whisper.

Then I see it all in slow motion the room spins and all I hear are the pounding of his fists and my screams crying out. I crouch as far into the corner as I can my arms locked around my knees trying to protect myself. He's out of control his fists hitting harder and harder my cries turning into a whimper of defeat.

Eventually, he stops and we sit there slumped in exhaustion. I stay cowering in the corner, the blood running down my legs, he looks less angry more annoyed." is it over" the voice in my head says.

He gets up and passes me a towel, for a moment I stay huddled in my spot. I look into his eyes he seems different he gestures the towel to me again and I stretch out a hand to take it from him. He stands there watching me, I feel ashamed and

19

want him to revert his gaze but he doesn't, instead, he wraps the towel around me and kisses my forehead. I wince and pull away, he scoops me up and carries me to the bed, gently placing me on it.

His head is slightly bowed "I'm sorry" he says quietly. I look at him and say nothing.

Steve walks away heading to the kitchen, I think maybe he feels ashamed I'm not sure. A Few minutes later he is back with two glasses of whiskey, he offers one to me"here drink this" I take the glass and do as he says. the warm alcohol burns my throat, but I gulp it down and place the glass on the bedside table. He sits next to me and we stay there in silence whilst he sips on his whiskey, I hear the hallway clock ticking for what seems like an eternity, my mind is elsewhere, maybe contemplating his next move.

"Let's get that wet towel off you, you don't want to catch a cold and it's making the bed damp" his voice is smoother now and more caring. I do as he asks and pull the bed covers up over my nakedness. I just want to sleep now I'm exhausted from crying and fighting everything hurts and my head is pounding."Let's take a look at those cuts and bruises"no mention of my obvious bleeding I guess he thinks I'm on my period.

he takes some cotton wool and ointment and tries to pull back the covers, I grip them tightly my head turned away in shame I don't want him to look at me. I disgust myself. He pulls harder "let me help you" his voice is soothing. He dabs the ointment onto the cotton wool and then onto my skin, I'm so confused I don't understand and the tears begin to roll down my cheeks. He wipes them away with his thumb "I really am sorry, god you make me so mad!"

20

"I'm sorry too" my voice ashamed of myself for apologizing."I need some you know things" I say looking at the bloodied stain on the bed.

"I will get you something to help" and he trots off to the bathroom like nothing happened. He hands me a sanitary towel and some knickers and watches as I place the towel in between my legs and pull the knickers up.

"Here take these it will help" handing me two blue pills. I swallow them down and then wriggle back under the covers, my body turned away from him. He nestles next to me and begins stroking my hair"you really are so beautiful" he says over and over and I drift off to sleep.

When I first wake the next morning the sun is streaming in through the window. I peek at him laying next to me, he looks so peaceful when he sleeps, his hair is tousled, his chest gently rising and falling as he breathes. And for a moment I long to touch him for him to hold me and caress me as if I have woken from a dream, but then I look at myself and feel my bruised body and tears roll down my cheek. The blood has leaked all over the bed and I think about stabbing him right there and then while he sleeps, I walk to the kitchen and take a knife from the drawer. Its blade is long and glistening in the sunlight and I think yes you can do this just fucking kill him. But my senses tell me how stupid I am to think I could stab him and get away with it, what if he wakes whilst I'm hovering over him with the intent of ending the bastards life.No I can't do it, so I just dig the tip of the knife into my thigh, enough to make it bleed and I feel some sort of release from my torment. I leave my side of the bed uncovered revealing the dark red patch and then go shower away my shame.

The coming days consist of sleeping and reading whiling

away the hours and minutes he brings me cups of tea, toast, or fruit in an attempt to get me to eat. I stay in my fluffy oversized sweater in some bid to offer my self-comfort, and a pair of leggings I usually wear to the gym. We do not mention the previous day's events.

The bruises begin to fade and the bleeding subsides, but my mind is lost in a dark void of pain and torment, I cry a lot and he holds me and I cannot understand what I am here for.

The next day I awake early, the birds are chirping their dawn chorus I feel light on my feet and somewhat happy. He seems happy too."You're smiling at last" his voice is content.

"I'm glad as I need you today, we have a client booked for you", his voice is casual but not friendly. He looks me in the eye, a look I have grown to recognize that says don't argue. I smile a fake smile, he kisses me on the forehead"good girl" he kisses me again on the lips, he is urgent telling me he needs me, my resilience subsides like a wave crashing over the shore, the heat between my thighs surging through my body. I kiss him hard and wantonly, his hand slips between my thighs, a moan slips out, I want him to take me there and then. Grabbing my legs he pulls me down and straddles me pushing himself inside me, I let out an urgent cry, why does he make me feel this way?

My legs are wrapped around his waist my hands pushing on his buttocks guiding him in deeper, I feel my pleasure increasing. I have no control my body is taking over "fuck me" I call out "god I need you!"and he flips me onto all fours and pushes deeper inside me, harder and faster our bodies in perfect rhythm with each thrust my moans becoming louder and more urgent. I feel myself approaching climax and at this moment I am completely surrendered to him. He comes too his grip tightening on my waist as he pushes himself to climax, and then he lets out a moan saying my name.

We collapse in a heap our bodies glistening with sweat our hearts pumping our breath deep and exhausted. A few moments go by I lie there feeling serene in the afterglow of our lovemaking.

He breaks the silence "I need to go out, Eddie will be here shortly we have business to attend to" I'm saddened I do not want him to leave me, he sees the look on my face "I won't be long" he reassures. My stomach is churning "can't you just stay here with me today" I'm trying not to sound too desperate.

"Why don't you go see the girls and I will get Eddie to pick you up later," he says it in a way that's an order rather than an option.

I suppose I will have to go back soon and anyway the girls haven't seen me all week, I wonder if they are worried about me?

But I know the answer to this is yes.

As I knocked on the door of the house I had shared for the past year I was not glad to be there. I didn't need all their questions and sympathy.

Molly(number 2 we call her)*this will be explained at a later date

came to the door scantily clad in just her knickers and a sheer babydoll, this was usual for her."Eva" she shrieked

"omg, what the fuck happened to you we haven't seen you all week!"

"Is he here" her voice concerned as she stuck her head out the door and took a look around."No" I said "It's just me" and I slip past her into the hallway. Number 2 checked again then came in and closed the front door behind her.

The others came rushing downstairs all huddling around

me with a cross between excitement and wanting to hear the latest gossip.

I slumped to the floor it was too overwhelming and the tears began to stream down my cheeks.

Clara(number 4)puts her arm around me."Get her a drink!" shouted Harry(number 6)we called her Harry for short as her name was Harriet

Clara tiptoed off to the kitchen, she always walked like that in her bare feet. reminded me of when I was a child pretending to walk in my mother's high heels

Harry put her arm around me as we walked to the front room the others following.

"what's he done to you this time?" and she took hold of my hand. the girls all sat around waiting for me to speak.

"It's ok I'm fine," I said not even believing it myself

"Well, I'm not accepting that! the Bastard!" Harry spoke with distaste."Well I'm assuming it was him and not a client, only I know you were supposed to be with a client"

"I don't want to talk about it, it's just the usual stuff you know" I spoke and the girls all nodded with understanding.

Clara returned from the kitchen with a large brandy."Here drink this" she said offering the glass out to me. I took it and gulped it down

Pru (number 1)and Molly (number 2)were whispering together looking concerned."Guys, I really will be ok, honestly, I can handle him, we all know how he gets, let's just have some fun as I expect we are all working later?" I tried to make light of it and spoke cheerily.

"What about you know, did it work or is there still a problem? Harry asked concerned

I really wanted to change the subject but at the same time

I wanted to be held and cared for and able to tell them about the baby, but we all knew the score it was best to just get on with things.

"It's done ok I don't want to talk about it ever!" my voice clear "Why don't I do your hair and makeup for late" chirped Harry(number 6)we called her Harry for short as her name was Harriet

Clara tiptoed off to the kitchen, she always walked like that in her bare feet. reminded me of when I was a child pretending to walk in my mother's high heels

Harry put her arm around me as we walked to the front room the others following.

"what's he done to you this time?" and she took hold of my hand. the girls all sat around waiting for me to speak.

"It's ok I'm fine," I said not even believing it myself

"Well, I'm not accepting that! the Bastard!" Harry spoke with distaste."Well I'm assuming it was him and not a client, only I know you were supposed to be with a client"

"I don't want to talk about it, it's just the usual stuff you know" I spoke and the girls all nodded with understanding.

Clara returned from the kitchen with a large brandy."Here drink this" she said offering the glass out to me. I took it and gulped it down

Pru (number 1)and Molly (number 2)were whispering together looking concerned."Guys, I really will be ok, honestly, I can handle him, we all know how he gets, let's just have some fun as I expect we are all working later?" I tried to make light of it and spoke cheerily.

"What about you know, did it work or is there still a problem? Harry asked concerned

I really wanted to change the subject but at the same time

I wanted to be held and cared for and able to tell them about the baby, but we all knew the score it was best to just get on with things.

"It's done ok I don't want to talk about it ever!" my voice clear "Why don't I do your hair and makeup for later" chirped Harry. She was the oldest I think at 22 she tended to mother us. I suppose it was also because the time she had spent with him gave her more knowledge of the way things were.

We spent the rest of the afternoon and early evening in our loungewear watching chick flicks and giving each other beauty treatments. You see our days were mainly spent waxing or fake tanning. We had our own sunbed so we could keep our tans topped up only Pru stayed lily-white. I hadn't had any pubic hair since Steve decided to shave it off after he finally convinced me never to return home. He said it made me more pleasing to clients who wanted a young girl. Bloody pervs I used to think to myself.

It was like a family, but not, they were not really my friends but all we had was each other, and in this cold and dark world that was everything.

As time ticked on the house became a bustle of girls pruning themselves, laughing, and chatting as they got ready for the evening.

"Come on Vicky, you need to get ready!" Harry shouted down the stairs. I really did not want to move but I had no choice I had to work.

"Coming" I shouted back as I got up and walked up the stairs.

Pru and Molly were in their room together singing into their hairbrushes to some 80s track. They were dressed in knickers stockings and suspenders. I smiled as I walked past their room, they had each other and I knew they were close and had a special bond. Molly was tall at least 5'8 with brunette hair and the most amazing pair of tits. Her hair fell in big curls onto her shoulders her breasts bouncing around as she danced and sang into her hairbrush, She really was beautiful to look at and I loved to look at her. Her green eyes always sparkled even though I could see her darkness. Pru on the other hand was petite and blonde, her hair cut into a bob, her breasts were smaller and pert with rose-pink nipples, she was strong and confident in her body.

Mine was the room next to theirs. I was the only one who did not share a room as Clara and Harry shared the third room together. I was glad as Clara was so messy and seemed to take over the whole room.

I went in and sat at the dressing table looking at myself in the mirror, not sure what I was expecting to see back."Who am I?" I started to undress and stood looking at myself for a moment, I was beautiful so youthful and puerile long red hair with a slight wave that fell to my waist, my large breasts blossoming like a flower my appearance fresh and full of vigor. I was a size eight to ten but had curves that every girl would die for and legs that had been talked about since I was in school. I checked myself out in the mirror ashamed of what I saw, my beauty spoilt by the bruising.

I was uneasy being on my own so went into Clara and Harry's room. Clara was sat at the end of her bed moisturizing her legs. I picked up the discarded clothes as I went in and opened the lid of the laundry basket and threw them in."I don't know how you ever find anything in this mess" I said with a laugh. I could see Clara watching me as I stood by the wardrobe mirror naked. The bruises were still apparent. Clara slammed the bottle of lotion onto the bed.

27

"For fucks sake Eva you said it was nothing! that's not nothing!!I bloody knew it!" she was talking loudly and Harry appeared in the doorway."Stop looking at me, it won't help, at least it wasn't one of you" and a tear began to roll down my cheek. I was annoyed I needed to keep it together. Clara grabbed hold of my wrist, I shook her off "I need to get ready, I can't let him down again, I don't want the punishment and neither do any of you, now help me get ready or it will be you he's gunning for!" my voice was angry but hurt.

Although I knew they cared the room fell silent, it was just the way it was we got on with it, anyway who were we to question his methods. It was hopeless and the truth behind the laughter we shared was more than any of us could really bear. The silence was a communication we all understood.

The car beeped its horn outside around 7:30 pm. Eddie was Steve's driver and took most of us to meet clients. I got into the back seat we glanced at each other in the rearview mirror but said nothing. He stopped outside a small hotel and escorted me up to the room."Now don't forget he has rather different tastes but you know what to do, oh and pick up the cash first should be £500" I nod in obedience and take a deep breath. I am about to knock on the door when Eddie stops me."here" he says reaching in his pocket and taking out a small bag of white powder."A little pick me up to help" He takes his keys from his pocket dips the end in the bag producing a heap of the white stuff. I lean forward and snort it up my nostril."Thanks, Eddie"

I knock on the door ready with my fake smile to greet him, my head just saying to itself get it done!

I take another deep breath and I'm in the room. Well, she is anyway as this is not really me.

My mind and body are totally focused on what I'm there to

do, although my mind keeps drifting off to someplace nice.

He stands by the window. tall dark-haired and well dressed apart from the tie he has loosened from his collar. I walk towards him."get on the bed" he demands. I do as he asks. He stands at the end of the bed looking at me."mm very nice, please take off your dress!" and he continues to watch me his eyes taking in every detail of me. I struggle with the zip and in his frustration, he unzips me and I wriggle free exposing my lace bra and knickers. my breasts swell over the top of the lace my nipples protruding through the sheer fabric, my mound visible through the lace of my knickers.

"Do you want me to unzip you?" I ask confidently as I can already see his erection through his trousers.

"No I want to take some pictures of you first" and he takes out

a camera from the side table.

I hated this, but I tried smiling convincingly.

"Lie back" and all I hear is click-click as he takes several

photos."Put your arms above your head for me" he demonstrates with hand gestures

I do so. He puts the camera down on the bed takes off his tie and ties my wrists together.

"I want you to turn and look at me"

I turn my head in his direction ."Okay that's great" his voice is breathy as his arousal grows. He puts the camera back on the bedside table ."now you can unzip me and suck off my dick"

I sit up on the bed, he moves forward and kneels in front of me, I reach for his belt and loosen it then unzip his trousers and reach in to release his already throbbing cock.I lick it up and down teasing his tip, and make small moans of pleasure. I take him into my mouth, slowly at first then more urgently and faster, he pushes down on my head forcing himself deeper into my throat until I nearly gag, and then releases me.

He takes his cock from my mouth and pushes me back onto the bed, my legs splayed apart."remove your panties" he demands his voice breathy and husky. I slide them down over my buttocks and kick them off, my pussy is already wet I open my legs to show him.

He hits me in the face my eye is bloody a swollen, he hits me again and again I scream with the pain. He's on top of me breathing hard and sweating and cursing.

He was hurting me...... "Don't fuck with me !" The rest is just a blur

I am eight

Gagged and bound I'm led down the steps into the basement. A group of men stand there and my legs begin to buckle beneath me, surely I'm not to be offered up to all of them, I'm horrified and afraid. But the question has already been answered in my mind and I know that my life will be changed forever.

I'm already struggling and crying out as he takes me to the mattress on the floor, Steve removes the gag and unties my wrists. I could try and run but I know I can't.

"You don't have to do this I will do whatever you want!" I scream in desperation at him, but the first man is already pulling down my trousers and I'm kicking trying to stop him but the others hold me down.

"You got a real fighter here," he says. "she will calm down eventually, you'll see"

I don't want this to happen I want to go home. And for the first time, I want my mother. I cry out pleading with him but he's already on top of me my knickers torn off and discarded like a rag. I try to pull away but they are too powerful I'm hoping Steve will tell them to stop but he's just standing there watching with great interest.

The third then the fourth I wonder how long this will go on my throat is dry from screaming I'm still fighting with every ounce of strength I have in me hoping they will stop.

I'm sore the brutal thrusts feel like they will tear me apart, my knees are red raw, they pull me around like a doll. My mind slips away trying to find some nice memory to cling to but it's blank.

When the fourth stops I take a moment to gather myself but then the fifth comes and flips me onto my stomach."God no not in there" I scream as he forces himself into my anus. The pain sears through me like a hot poker but I still fight as best I can, and Steve still stands and watches.

Number six and seven come together and I'm beginning to lose all hope I know I cannot stop them and my screams have died down to sobbing I want it to end.

"Why are you doing this to me, please stop your hurting me" I'm sobbing my chest so tight I can't breathe only take a shallow breath, and at last as the next approaches, I stop. My voice is strangled not even a whisper and inside I'm screaming so loud the whole street would hear.

There is silence I lay there while he thrusts into me not a sound from my lips, my body like a piece of meat, I have lost all ability to fight them and I give my body to them

I am paralyzed there in that room and darkness comes over me tying me in a knot and there is no humanity to be found.

When he had finished the men headed upstairs chatting and joking, Steve plants a kiss on my forehead "Good girl, now that wasn't that bad was it" and he smiles and walks upstairs, I hear the key turn in the lock and all there is the dark.

Down in that cellar, a girl had been born full of pure rage and anger, continually tormented and too dangerous to let out she wanted to wreak havoc everywhere and cause destruction and ultimately her own death. She was number eight.

And so it begins my life in the world of darkness and depravity only a couple of years ago I was full of ambition and hope of a better life. I was always striving for something I didn't have and now the realities of that endeavor have led me to this torturous place I'm supposed to call home.

I sometimes think how different things would have been if had not been so eager to enter into adulthood and lose my virginity if had not wanted to pursue the arousal I felt that needed to be fulfilled. IF had become the biggest word in my dictionary. The days of my intellect and extensive vocabulary, my gift with music and my singing voice, the aura that shone around me, and my carefree soul which had made my friends full of envy had been stripped away. I'm sure they would not now be envious of my ability to blow a man off with just a few strokes or that I had been fucked in every hole by every shape and size and every degree of man.No, they would not they would surely laugh and think I was a slut.!And they would be right I was just a dirty whore who spent most of her days performing sexual acts for the highest bidder.

But there was another side to this the girl whose presence made him grow weak the girl that he adored who adored him back she was something special, something I cannot describe, but an addiction craved by many.

In reality life was tough and brutal filled with constant pain and injury the favorite being made of old worn brown leather. There it was looped through his jeans like a gun in its holster, the buckle glistening as the sunlight caught it. It was not a thing of beauty but a constant weapon ready to be released from its holster and bring down pain on my bare body. We became quite accustomed to each other to a point where I could sense its imminent release. This was the tool of my obedience but resistance over time made my obedience subside.

I was sitting across the breakfast bar from him eating dinner, again a thing that became less frequent until eventually the need for food was at the bottom of my survival.

I sat watching him shovel the spaghetti into his mouth and then wash it down with a glass of red. I had been chasing the fork around the plate as I had little or no appetite. I sipped on my glass of wine watching him with great interest like I was learning every inch of him, every line and wrinkle every hair follicle, the way his lips smiled, the light in his green eyes, the vein in his neck protruding when he was angry. I was mesmerized watching, learning his every move and then he looked up from his plate. "What are you looking at?" he glared

"Eat your food," he said pointing to my plate. "I'm not that hungry thanks" and I took another sip of wine. Steve was up off his stool before I had time to gulp it down and had snatched the glass from my hand sending red wine everywhere, and grabbing hold of the back of my head had pushed my face hard into my plate. "Eat you ungrateful bitch!" he shouted. I was so shocked I just sat there spaghetti all over my face. I took a napkin and wiped it away my tears stinging my eyes trying not to let them fall down my cheek.

"Go get the belt!" he commanded. I stayed sat where I was and he shouted again "Go get the belt"

The said belt was usually in its holster kept safe in the belt loops of his jeans but at this very moment, it resided in our bedroom where he had undressed. I pushed my stool out from the breakfast bar and walked towards the bedroom, Steve followed me.

"Can we not do this please" my voice shaking. "I don't understand what I did wrong?"I'm sobbing now unable to control my emotions. Steve just stands there waiting.

I take the belt from his jeans and gingerly hand it to him. I can see the look of pleasure on his face as he takes it from me and cracks it loudly.

Next, I take the handcuffs from the bedside drawer and put them on my wrist locking the other to the hook on the bedroom wall. I stand looking over my shoulder crying waiting for the first strike, but in my obedience, I have cuffed myself whilst still clothed. He approaches me and yanks my shorts and knickers down and pulls my t-shirt up over my

35

head.

"Please don't do it "but I don't finish what I'm saying when the first strike hits my left buttock sending a hot burning pain through me and before I have time to regain composure the second has hit me again across the buttocks. I grit my teeth trying not to cry out, my legs beginning to wobble. He strikes me harder now across the back and the cry comes from my mouth pain like red hot pokers each time with more force the belt cutting into my skin. I am not counting I wish it to end I am begging him to stop now I can't take another strike I cannot stand from the pain I'm enduring. He strikes me again this time with the buckle end catching me on my buttock. I scream loudly. "PLEASE NO MORE" but another two strikes come leaving me red raw and bleeding clinging onto the hook in the wall for support.

I hang there and think to myself how I'd never eat spaghetti again.

Life's a beach

My most favourite thing is the sea, and at any opportunity to dip my toes in I would be there.

I'm sure this was due to living in a small seaside town during my childhood where I spent most of my days at the beach swimming in the sea.

It was a gloriously sunny day in July and after a few weeks of hard work, Steve said we could have a day out.

Days out were a rarity and something not to be taken for granted, and I loved the escape they gave me. A time I could sort of feel free , be normal and take in the fresh air.

"Let's go to the beach "I shrieked with excitement. "We can get a proper tan and I can swim in the sea and then we can get fish n chips, oh come on you lot Harry tell them it will be great" my excitement hard to contain.

"Ok calm down Eva we will go whos in," said Harry.

"I will come but only if I can bring the baby she's never been to the seaside "Clara shouted from the kitchen. Pru and Molly were in the lounge dozing on the sofa. "No thanks we're exhausted," said Molly "And I don't want to get sand in places where it shouldn't be thank's" replied Pru.

In the next hour, we were driving through the main road, and we were on our way to the beach, which is actually my favorite place in the world so far. The sea water was blue and beautiful as it sparkled in the warm sun. There were a few people here and there on the beach. Some were busy playing tennis, while a few kids were building sandcastles just for fun. There were at least three or six people for the most, already bathing in the clear, blue sea water. By the time, we had gotten out of the car, I was already excited to go into the water and enjoy a fine sea bath.

Clara set up the blanket and took Rachel from her pushchair and sat her on it. We had a large golf umbrella for some shade so she didn't get too hot. I kicked off my sandals pulled my top off and wriggled out of my denim shorts, my bikini already on under my clothes, I grab Harry's hand and run frantically towards the sea screaming with excitement.

The water was cool and wonderful I could have stayed there until it was time for us to pack up and go home. Harry and I were splashing about and giggling wildly it felt so refreshing to do something so normal, I pulled her to me and kissed her then pushed her head under the waves. "Catch me if you can" I yelled as her head bopped back up and I began to swim out towards the horizon. She swims out too until we can no longer see our legs.

"We should go back now Eva I think we have swum far enough and I want to get a tan"

"ok", I reply reluctantly. So we swim back towards the shore.

We head up towards where Clara is sitting, Rachel playing with her toys in the shade. I flick my wet hair at Clara and she shrieks out but she's laughing.

"You should go in, we can watch Rachel "

"Maybe in a bit "Clara replies.

I lay back looking up at the blue sky the sun beating down on my glistening skin and I feel truly happy.

Very few appreciate the wonderful feeling of the powdery sand between your toes, or the blissful sensation of the cool waves crashing against your ankles, legs, waist.

The sand glistened, drenched in parts, and burning in others. The water was ebbing and the waves calmly followed. I watched for what seemed like hours and wished we never had to leave. Rachel's cries brought me back from my daydream, she was too hot and tired so I offered to take her for a stroll in the pushchair to get her off to sleep. I slipped my denim shorts back on over my damp bikini bottoms and clambered up the beach dragging Rachel's pushchair up onto the promenade.

Watching all the hustle and bustle of adults and children walking along the promenade I felt like I could be one of them. I smiled as I passed them proudly pushing Rachel along and stopped for small talk when people said how cute she was or hasn't she got your eyes. I could just blend in with the rest of the world, maybe I could just run off, but then I'd be without Harry and I couldn't take Rachel from Clara I wouldn't put her through the pain of losing her. I wished I could make Steve want me and only me, that I could be enough and we could leave this life behind. If I had a child with him he would want to do that. But these were just childish fantasies.

Rachel was sleeping soundly now the motion of the wheels on her pushchair sending her off into peaceful sleep. I had better get back before anyone thought I had run off.

Up ahead was an icecream stand I felt into the pocket of my

shorts and pulled out the scrunched-up tenner I had put in there that morning.

3 Mr whippy with a flake, please. The icecream seller looked up and smiled. He was young and handsome his tanned skin making his blue eyes stand out, I smiled back a flirtatious smile for I had seen how he looked at me . He handed me the three cones and I fumbled to hold them giving him the scrunched up tenner his hand lightly touching mine as he took it and rang it up on the till. My conscience told me to stop my flirtation and get back to Clara and Harry. I took the change and headed off three cones in one hand that were melting fast in the summers heat and the other trying desperately to steer Rachels pushchair.

I walked back to the spot where we were sitting and shouted to the girls for some help. Clara trunched across the hot sand and took the pushchair from me so I could carry the icecream

"Thanks," they said as I handed them an ice cream each and plonked myself down on the blanket. I licked the dripping ice cream from my hand.

We spent the rest of the afternoon letting the suntan our pale bodies and dipping Rachels tiny toes in the sea. It was heaven just us three being girls being friends sharing a day at the beach, I didn't want it to end.

Clara ordered fish and chips and we sat on the sea wall eating out of the container with our little wooden forks and throwing the occasional chip to a swooping seagull, and then it was time to return home but I was smiling and I was happy for the day we had had for the sand between my toes and the memories.

Eddie was waiting "come on girls that's enough fun for one day" and he opened the car door for us to get in. Clara sat in the back with Rachel in her arms still soundly sleeping, Harry sat next to her so I got in the front passenger seat. Eddie smiled, he liked to be close to me, I smiled back. My head rested on the headrest of the car I was tired from the heat and could see I was quite burnt from it. Eddies hand touched my thigh I placed mine on top of his checking the rearview mirror for signs that the girls had seen. Luckily they were both asleep and so I allowed Eddie's hand to stay there until they stirred. I gazed out of the window at the setting sun watching the flickering of light through the trees and hedgerows as we drove home, and I wished this day would not end. My eyes were heavy I allowed sleep to take over and drifted off dreaming of a better world.

In the cellar

Steve grabs me by my hair I grip onto his hands to stop him from wrenching my hair from my scalp."PLEASE I'm SORRY I won't DO IT AGAIN, I PROMISE PLEASE! STEVE STOP! You're HURTING ME, DON'T PUT ME DOWN THERE" I am screaming and pleading in desperation to change his course.!

"I promise you, I'm sorry really just not in there" my pleas fall on deaf ears. He drags me towards the cellar door. I kick my legs and twist my body with all my strength trying to free myself, I am screaming uncontrollably every ounce of my being helpless to his goal. He is silent his eyes glazed and wide like a wild beast, I try lashing out in a last ditched attempt to free myself my fists punching into the air, trying to hit him or something. I manage to grab onto the door frame my fingers and nails digging into it with all my strength. He releases his hold on my hair to grab my arm and pry my fingers from the frame. This is my opportunity I kick my legs at him kicking him in the face. It takes him by surprise and he staggers backward, I get onto my hands and knees trying to clamber onto my feet to run for the front door but he grabs my ankle and pulls me down."You fucking whore!" he shouts at me his voice is so chilling it rips at my very core. He has me by the waist now and I'm punching and kicking with all my might exhausted sobs coming from my mouth."please" his grip is tight and he ignores my plea.

The door to the cellar is open in front of me my time out for breaking the rules and I'm filled with terror, he can see it in my eyes, my face is streaked with makeup and tears my hair stuck to my face, he pushes me towards the door I cannot fight and I am tumbling down the stairs hitting my head on the way. The door slams and the key is turned.

I lay on the cold concrete floor rage and fear consuming me I am out of control I can't breathe and scratch at my throat as if I'm suffocating. I am crying loudly and uncontrollably louder than I have ever cried before. My heart is pounding in my chest "please let me out I can't breathe" I whimper. No reply comes there is only silence.

It's dark and damp with a musty smell and I can hardly see. I rub my eyes and wipe the tears and snot from my face with the back of my hand.it's still gloomy and dark in there and all I can make out is shapes so I throw my arms out at anything in my path crashing shelving units full of old tins of paint to the floor. He will come now, I tell myself. BUT NOTHING! This place is my own internal hell since I was branded number eight it was the last place on earth to be shut alone in the dark.

I am in a frenzy making as much noise and destruction as I can alone in that dark damp place but he doesn't come and I end up exhausting myself.

I curl up in a ball my tear-stained cheeks hot and flushed my throat raw and dry. I realize my hands are bruised and sore and I'm cold. In complete exhaustion, I hold onto myself and close my eyes tightly so I cannot see the dark. I sleep I don't know for how long as all sense of time has vanished. I wipe the dry snot and tears away with my t-shirt. My body aches partly from the struggle and partly from lying on the cold floor. It's a struggle to move my body feels like a dead weight, I try to get to my feet but my legs are like jelly. There's stuff strewn everywhere and I can see a small amount of light coming from a narrow window on the far side. I clamber towards it to see if there is a way out but there is too much junk in front of it and I do not have the energy. I will wait for the door to open, I'm sure he will open it any minute.

My throat is dry and I'm thirsty, I need water, he will come soon I'm sure. I sit in the same spot gazing up at the door listening for any sound of movement. How much time has passed by I'm unsure, but my bladder is now aching and I need to pee badly. I pace up and down counting in my head and singing to myself trying to distract me from my bladder. I wait and wait…nothing "Steve " I call my voice hoarse and thin "Let me out please"

All there is silence and I really do have to pee, my bladder throbbing more and more I look for something to relieve myself in but to my horror there is nothing and I really need to pee now. I feel so humiliated but I crouch in the corner and peel my knickers down, as I squat the hot stream of urine splashes up from the concrete floor on to my legs and feet I feel ashamed and dirty my degradation stabbing my heart like a hot poker. I pull my knickers back up and step over the puddle of urine.

I rack my brain trying to think of a way to be released, but my mind is just a jumble of thoughts and feelings. I sit and sob to myself rocking backward and forwards. I just want to die.

The next few hours are spent between periods of banging my fists profusely on the door until my knuckles bleed or screaming out until my head is sore. My energy is zapped. In the dark I envision him sitting upstairs laughing, ignoring me. I bet he is enjoying this I tell myself. I begin to see things in the dark him standing there and looking at me but it's my mind playing tricks on me. I have to get out! but I have already given in to the realization that release is not coming soon. I hold myself again and sob the hours ticking away, I can almost hear an imaginary clock ticking in my mind. I kept on whispering "I am not alone" until I had a sore throat. I'm thirsty now my lips are chapped and dry and I have no saliva. I drift in and out of sleep.

Sometime later............ i hear the key turn in the door, or is my mind playing tricks on me. Yes, it's my imagination I tell myself. I stay still and open one eye to take a peek I'm too afraid to look and be disappointed. I'm blinking in the light, I rub both eyes can it be? yes, the door is open and the light from upstairs is streaming in. My stomach churns. I hear footsteps on the steps down into the cellar and close my eyes tight my heart pounding in my throat I do not want to open

46

my eyes and see him. I'm shaking now.

"Eva come," he says I know his voice and open my eyes to see him standing there his arm is outstretched offering me his hand, but I cannot seem to move. He helps me to my feet but my legs buckle underneath me, I'm a wreck I feel ashamed of myself, he looks around and mutters to himself then scoops me up and carries me up the steps.

"What have you done to yourself? I can't leave you for 5 minutes without you smashing the place up!" his voice is angry but caring at the same time.

I cling to him as he carries me so glad of being freed and I don't want to let him go. I look down at myself my hands and knees are black my t-shirt covered in dirt makeup and snot my knicker's smell of dried pee. I feel ashamed.

"I hope we have an understanding now?" he questions me and I nod in agreement.

A tear stings my eye and rolls down my cheek I wipe it away quickly. don't cry I tell myself.

He escorts me to the bathroom and I stand there uncomfortably whilst he turns the dial for the shower and waits for the water to warm up."lift your arms up" this is an instruction so I do as instructed and he lifts my t-shirt up and over my head revealing my naked breasts, I cover them immediately with my hands uncomfortable within my own skin. Next, he takes my piss-stained knickers off and I step out of them, my head bowed down in such shame it overwhelms me ."get in" he instructs

I get in, the hot water is a welcome sense on my skin, I put my face up to the showerhead and let it wash over me drinking some of it in and pushing my hair back off my face. He has stripped off and is now standing naked behind me, he touches my hair smoothing it backwards so it falls down my back. then he squirts the shampoo onto his palm and begins to massage it into my scalp and down the length of my hair. His touch is electric it courses through my entire being and I revel in the closeness. I want him so badly he makes me feel weak and my legs buckle under me. He catches me and holds me his naked body pressed against mine. he turns me to face him, my head still hung with shame I don't want him to look at me like this. He lifts my chin and wipes the tear stains from my cheeks with his thumb. I stop him for a moment taking hold of his wrist, but then he looks at me and we start to kiss. I'm like a desperate child wanting to be fed, he plays with my nipple and my hand reaches for his already hard cock.I begin to stroke it my eyes telling him I want him, I cry my need for him is so overwhelming.

He holds me for a moment seeing the pain and lust in my eyes then penetrates me. I gasp as he enters me my lips not yet wet but as he continues I soon reciprocate with gentle rocking of my hips and little moans of pleasure. His hands are around my throat as he thrusts harder into me his grip tightening until I feel I can't breathe, the memory of the last 2 days washed away. We fuck with neediness and urgency with desperation for each other's touch and release of orgasm. He is forceful but not hurting me, I smell the muskiness of him and feel the hardness of him inside me. I can feel my orgasm building "please I'm gonna cum" I moan, tears falling down my cheeks from the sheer emotion of the last few days. He thrusts into me deeper and we both climax together my hands gripping his buttocks my nails biting into his flesh. My climax leaves me with a series of moans and loud cries and I hear him laugh."God girl you wanted that bad, didn't you?" he snorts, my head is on his chest still holding him."yes" I breathe" yes"

I'm so exhausted and ashamed of myself for wanting him so badly. We wash, I cry a little but try not to let it out, he won't want to hear it. I look down at myself bruised and battered my bruised knuckles and sigh.

"Mmm," he says half cross half laughing."not sure how I will explain that! but you did this to yourself, you stupid girl!"

"I'm sorry" and the words leave my lips before I even have the chance to think."I just didn't want to be left down there, I hate it when you leave me" and the tears begin to roll down my cheeks I cannot contain my sadness.

"Well if this is what your gonna do every time I will have to tie you up so you can't hurt yourself!" his voice is abrupt. I think to myself that I won't be going in there again. He grabs two towels and we dry ourselves in silence.

'Every day it was a survival. And I thought, "I'll be extra good today" because I didn't want to go in there again alone in the dark with all those demons tormenting my mind. But you know what, it doesn't matter how good I was, I still ended up in there a lot.'

I just want to forget what's happened and everything to be normal between us again, so I tell myself that obedience is the key I will do everything he tells me from now on until he forgives me. And for the next few weeks, I am obedient as fuck, I do everything he wants, see every client, make two of those horrible porn films, cook every meal, clean the flat, and have the best sex ever. I never complain or let him see my looks of disdain, I just get on with things.

Ok so that's not quite the truth, I hate every minute and use cocaine and alcohol to get me through I'm a whole different person now. I'm actually quite good at giving men what they desire whatever their fetish or fantasy is, and sometimes I really enjoy myself, even though the truth be told I'm numb to the feelings or pain now there is nothing but the outer shell of me. I spend my days eating, sleeping, fucking satisfying clients' needs, and staying home with the girls. If I wasn't being fucked or sleeping I was taking coke and drinking litre bottle of vodka.

I just wasn't made to be at someone's beck and call, I had had enough of obeying his commands or playing his games it was exhausting. I was in a dream state most of the time I couldn't sleep(if I did it was with one eye open) or eat I had lost about two stone in weight and my hip bones were sticking out.

For a time we laughed and joked and fucked together, he spent more and more time with me. Let me touch him whenever I wanted and that was all the time. I loved being this close to him, being in his arms, catching him looking at me and I would wonder what he was thinking about.? We seemed to be in tune with each other, we were closer than before and I think I even made him happy for a while.

But it wasn't to last. My good behavior bored him, he took his frustrations out on the girls who in turn took their frustrations out on me. They began to despise me I wasn't really one of them anymore, they felt I had special privileges and didn't have to work as hard as them, they said I had a bad attitude and thought I was above them somehow and that he should take me down a peg or two, get a new toy to play with so we could all get back to work.

I treated them with the contempt they gave me, I was paranoid thinking they were conspiring against me, trying to get Steve to think I was breaking rules or trying to leave. They wanted him to go back to mistreating me as he did them.

It wasn't fair!

My cocaine habit was becoming a problem I knew it and so did he. Sooner or later I was going to rebel all that hatred and fury was building up inside me, I felt like a caged animal.

You cant hide

"Where do you think you're going dressed like that? your body is for my eyes only" he joked

We were going to a club to meet some business associates, well friends and I was ecstatic, this was the first time I had been invited out. I wanted to be his eye candy and wanted them to know we were together.

At no point had he implied anything other than a few drinks with his friends at the club and a bit of business chat, so you can understand my shock and humiliation as the events unfold.

Eddie picked us up at 9:30 pm. He opened the rear passenger door and I got in giddy with excitement, I was happy we were laughing and chatting the whole journey.

Eddie pulled up outside the club and opened the rear passenger door. Steve stepped out and took my hand, my heart was racing as we walked through the door into the club.

The neon lights and the music made my heart dance, and then I saw the girls on stage and dancing on poles. "why have you brought me here?" I questioned him

He did not reply but tightened the grip on my hand and led me through the club to another room, I could hear jokes and laughter coming from inside as we approached.

Steve hesitated for a moment then took us through. I walked slightly behind him, my heart pounding in my chest and an uncomfortable feeling was building up inside me.

Just play it cool, these are his friends you need to make a good impression I told myself.

There were 8 men in the room which consisted of a couple of leather chesterfield sofas, two tables with armchairs, and a small bar area. Two of the men were perched at the bar deep in conversation. I smiled as we walked past. Three were sat around one of the tables playing poker and two were sitting on the sofa snorting lines of coke from the glass table in front of them…The room was softly lit with a few wall lights and lamps here and there. we sat down opposite the guys snorting ." this is the girl I've been telling you about" he said and motioned the two at the bar to come over and join us.

"Hi,I'm Eva," I said awkwardly holding out my hand to shake with there's. One of them stepped forward and went in for a full-on embrace ending in us bumping faces with each other and laughing awkwardly. Ok seems they like me.

"I need a drink" I chirped and got up to go to the bar with the guy that id just had the awkward encounter with."Two tequilas please" I motioned to the barman and stood there uncomfortably waiting for him to pour them, I was not good at small talk and needed a little dutch courage. I down both tequilas straight.

"Wow, you like a drink then" his friend laughed, and at that he motioned to the barman . "mike we will have another six please" then turning to me and his friend "let's get this party started" I looked around to see if I could get an acknowledgment or approval from Steve but he was not in the room. Oh well, I told myself he must be having that business chat he was talking about, and this gave me the green light to relax and enjoy myself after all these were his friends.

I perched on a stool between the two of them making small talk and lining up more shots. We were soon all laughing and joking together and I was relaxed and having fun. God knows where Steve was it seemed like he'd been gone ages and I thought we were supposed to spending the evening together. I told myself he probably wouldn't be much longer and that I should just have some fun and enjoy myself so when he comes back he will see us all getting along together. The drinks were flowing music was playing and I felt happy and alive.

I got off my stool and started to sway to the music." show us your moves then" one of them retorted

I started to dance my body feeling the rhythm of the music and moving in an expressive and erotic motion. Everyone seemed to be joining in and having fun cheering and laughing. I was perspiring now and feeling a little dizzy from all the shots so slumped onto one of the sofas. The coke was still in lines on the glass table and a guy was slumped on the opposite sofa. "mind if i" I gestured to the rolled-up twenty discarded on the table letting him know I was asking to do some. I bent forward and snorted the first line, and then another "that's better" I said out loud and went back off to join the others dancing. We were all gyrating against each other and I was loving every minute. I pulled the hem of my dress up a little higher and started to dirty dance and grind against one of the guy's legs. He was holding me by the waist I lent back letting my hair sway. He pulled me back up to him and we kissed.

I was completely lost in the moment my head giddy from the dancing, alcohol, and drugs. I was unaware of my surroundings and began to feel out of control. All of a sudden there was silence and someone was grabbing me and pulling me away. It was Steve he was furious his eyes dark hard and angry. "What the fuck are you doing?" I was giddy and confused and was finding it difficult to balance myself. "well?" he shouted

"I was just dancing" I slurred

"You're making a spectacle of yourself and me, I knew I shouldn't have brought you" he was furious and I was stuttering but no words came out.

"Let her stay she's not doing any harm and I thought you were gonna let us all fuck her anyway?" someone piped up.

This outburst increased his rage he flipped his eyes were glazed over he grabbed the guy by the throat choking him for a few moments and then let him go.

I was so humiliated and upset the words just came out.

"So I'm just a fucking whore for your friends to stick their dicks in" I shouted at him "well come on here I am" I gestured to the room stripping off my dress.

"For fucks sake Eddie get her home" Steve ordered to him, and with that Eddied had grabbed me by the waist and thrown me over his shoulder in a fireman's lift, I was kicking and screaming "YOU FUCKING BASTARD I HATE YOU!!"

We left by a side door me still flung over Eddie's shoulder muttering my disgust at having been removed from the party. The car was parked up, Eddie put me on my feet threw his jacket around me, and opened the rear passenger door." Get in" he pointed to me to get in

55

I was so drunk now and feeling sleepy my head flitting between being angry saying fuck you and worrying about what Steve would do to me. I just wanted to curl up in bed and feel sorry for myself. Eddie looked at me in the rearview mirror and shook his head.

I mumbled at him "I fucked up didn't I?" "yes Eva you did" he agreed.

"Look I'm not taking you back to his tonight I will take you home, but I'm only helping you this once!" he was softly spoken in a reassuring way.

"Thanks" I send my face ashamed and embarrassed.

It was getting light when we pulled up outside the house I shared with the girls. I must have dozed off for a bit and I felt horrendous. Eddie opened the car door and scooped me up and carried me in.

I had his suit jacket on and just my bra and knickers, my shoes I had kicked off my feet on the drive home. He took me upstairs and laid me on my bed and gently kissed my forehead.

"Thanks" I croaked

He pulled the throw from the end of the bed up and over me tucking me in, as he did so I realized I still had his jacket on and sat up to take it off. "here" I said " I have your jacket you'd better take it back. I took it off and handed it to him. He smiled at me.

"You didn't have to this, thank you" he sat on the end of the bed and started to say something but seemed to change his mind. "You'd better get some sleep" his voice was warm and comforting and I wanted him to keep talking to me.

"Will you just lie with me for a while, just till I fall asleep? please?" I begged him to stay and hold me for a while.

"Eva you know I can't, I've already done way too much." his

voice was firm

"Please just for a few minutes I feel terrible and no one will ever know" I promised him."Okay, but just for a minute" and he lay down next to me his arm across me.his fingers entwined in mine and we drifted off to sleep.

I awoke my heart was pounding, I was sweating and my head hurt to lift it off the pillow. Cocaine comedowns were so bad my body was aching and wrecked. Eddies arm was still across me, shit I startled myself what time is it! I glanced at the bedside clock it was gone 11 am. I leapt out of bed in a frantic panic" shit, shit, shit"

Eddie woke up rubbing his eyes." shit I'm in so much trouble now. you need to go!" I was shouting at him and collecting up his things. I passed him his jacket and trousers which he must have taken off at some point, and he hurried himself to get dressed, but it was too late I could hear the bellowing coming up the stairs "Is she here?" he sounded mad

"Oh fuck" I was starting to crumble, the door to my bedroom flung open and there was Steve looking absolutely furious, he saw Eddie trying to get his trousers on. "Steve you've got it wrong nothing happened," I said in a guilty way but trying to be reassuring. I stood there my legs were shaking"Are you going to cry now" his voice was sarcastic and belittling. He just glared at me and then went to speak to Eddie who had now managed to get his trousers on and fastened up.

"Did you enjoy her?" his voice was accusing. "Aye! was her tight little cunt nice?" he was getting angrier and angrier

"Boss nothing happened, I brought her home as you said and she was in a bad way so I didn't want to just leave her like that so I waited till she fell asleep and well I must have dozed off myself" his voice was very convincing. "I never touched her boss, I was just looking after her for you like you said, you know id never touch her" he assured.

"Just fuck off out of my sight" Steve shouted at him. Eddie grabbed his jacket and headed off out downstairs.

My stomach was churning I felt I was gonna be sick, I was contemplating his next move.

"Stay there! I will deal with you later" he snorted "you're mine I own you and don't you ever forget that! I can't do this anymore with you! is this how little you think of me? do I have to lock you in again until you learn? now I'm gonna have to hurt you, why are you so disobedient" and with that, he turned and went out the door.

I sighed with a little relief, I was off the hook for now. I sat on the end of the bed my head in my hands feeling sorry for myself. There was absolute chaos and noise coming from the rest of the upstairs, I could hear the opening and slamming of doors and drawers and shouting.

"Anything to hide in here, any other men you lot are hiding?!" he sounded really pissed off. I stayed perched on the end of my bed listening to the chaos unfolding and contemplating if I should just make a run for it while I could. My room was at the front of the property and overlooked the porch, I could easily climb out and down and no one would notice I was gone. I had crept out on many occasions before and sat there and watched the stars go by.

I have no choice I told myself it's going to be bad either way but at least I will have a few hours before the inevitable happens. I grab a t-shirt and a pair of gym leggings and hurriedly get dressed, scrabbling for a pair of trainers I had kicked under my bed sometime before. I grabbed the hoodie from the back of the chair and some cash from my bedside drawer(i always kept some just in case). I could still hear him shouting and the girls screaming back at him so now was my chance.

My heart was pounding, my head was pounding but it was now or never! I went to the window and slowly and quietly as I could opened the catch and flung the window wide open. I could feel the adrenaline and felt like my heart was gonna come out of my chest. I was afraid but exhilarated. I climb up on my chair and step one leg out onto the porch roof, well there's no going back now. I step out with the other leg and I'm there standing on the porch roof terrified but wanting to escape so badly it spurred me on. I turn and gently close the window behind me. I take one last second to pause and contemplate my choices but I can't go back now what if he sees me when I'm climbing back in, then I may as well be as good as dead! and before I realize it I've climbed down the fence and I'm running faster and faster across gardens down streets until my street is far away. Only then do I stop for breath and take a glance backward, and too my relief there is no one there.

But I knew I could not hide forever, he would find me probably sooner rather than later and I did not want to contemplate what my fate would be when he did.

I had nowhere to go. I wandered the streets in the middle of the night and I was scared.I find a doorway at the back of boots the chemist and huddle up in the corner and sleep.

Last night I dreamt I was me again. I was back in my parent's house with my siblings, watching TV on a Saturday night. My older sister braiding my just-washed hair. We would drink hot chocolate and stay up till late telling stories in the room we shared. My mother would tell us to turn the light out and go to bed, so we would whisper to each other in the dark until

59

we fell asleep. I would dream of the life I was going to have …..

Eddie spots me later that day sat at the bar, drunk and I know my freedom is short-lived. It's over now there's no escape. He sits down next to me his hand on my elbow. "Don't do it, Eddie, just let me go I will leave town and no one will ever see me again" I appeal to his softer nature.

"I have no choice Eva, I have to take you back" he looks genuinely sad. "Anyway you know you can't survive out here on your own with that pretty little face your gonna get into all kinds of trouble with no one to help you. You have no money nowhere to stay. are you gonna just prostitute yourself out here on the streets?it will be a hard life for you out here always looking over your shoulder." his words are bitter and harsh but I know he is right. I succumb to my fate and Eddie escorts me to the car, and for the first time in a long time, I wish I was already dead!

The drive home seems to take forever giving me way too much time for my mind to wander, the monsters building inside my head. We pull up outside the flat is in darkness which I should have realized was strange but I just felt relief that no one seemed to be home. I thought I would get up early and make breakfast and make myself look nice and maybe that would help calm the situation a little as if any of this was actually gonna change anything, but I had to try at least, yes that's what I would do.

Eddie follows me in in itself was unusual, but I assumed no one was home and he was just here to mind me. I do sense some unease with him, but shrug it off as my imagination and I'm actually rather tired and just want to sleep in my own bed. My mind is wandering so I decide to have a glass of wine in the hope it will help me to relax. I head into the kitchen still in darkness except for the soft glow of the under cupboard lighting. I open the fridge door there's half a bottle of chardonnay in the fridge door I pick up the bottle and gesture to Eddie "do you want a glass" I say "seeing as your obviously going to be keeping an eye on me!"He doesn't answer. "ok suit yourself I say and begin to pour myself a glass. Eddie is sat at the breakfast bar looking dark and silent, he's not in a talking mood I say to myself and turn to the fridge for a snack I'm hungry and I'm hoping there will be some leftovers to munch on. As I open the door I feel a punch to the back of my head knocking me cleanout.

I'm not sure how long I've been out for but when I come to I'm in the cellar, but it's not in darkness the light is on and there's a group of men standing in a circle. I try to regain my senses, am I dreaming, but the binding on my wrists tells me I'm not. I look shocked and frightened Steve is there too and I can hear sobbing but it's not me. then I see her she looks around 14 I would say a look of terror on her tear-stained face her hands tied her mouth gagged in the middle of the circle of men she's a year older I think than I was laying there on some old mattress, and I cry out in terror "NO!!"

Eddie ushers me towards the circle so I can see, I try to resist and turn my head away. "You will watch!"Steve orders

I'm filled with dread I do not want to see what's going to unfold, I can't watch I just can't.

"Please Steve you don't have to do this" Eddie has his hands on me keeping my head in the direction of the circle. The girl is sobbing her frightened eyes making contact with mine.

I'm frozen I cannot speak the horror I'm about to witness is more than I can bear I just want to die. "Kill me now please I don't want to be part of this, do it to me but not her please, take me" I beg them all not to do it. But the first man approaches the girl .she screams in fright as he pulls her underwear down and straddles her. I try to get away but I'm kneeling down my hands tied and Eddie forcing my head to watch. I can see Steve watching me as the horror unfolds he seems to be enjoying my anguish, and the man penetrates her, she screams and struggles, her eyes pleading to me to help her from her torment. she is raped by three men they fuck her throwing her around like a rag doll. when the second man tries to penetrate her analy I can see the look in her eyes her head is turned in my direction another man has his foot on the side of her head another holding her down whilst the third rips her apart and I just sit there and watch, her screams penetrate my very soul and tears stream down my face. I tell myself to do something but I know it's hopeless. This is the initiation and it's my fault that she is here, if I hadn't of runoff he wouldn't have needed to replace me. This is my punishment for thinking I could leave. I want them to stop, but not because I really care about what they are doing to her but because I can't stand it any longer.

When the fourth man approaches she succumbs to the inevitable and stops her crying, she accepts what is happening to her and the circle breaks leaving her in a heap on the floor and I say to her in my head welcome number 3.

Steve approaches me, the rest of them have left and gone upstairs to clean up.

"I feel nothing for you. Absolutely nothing!" I yell at him

"is that so?" his tone is amused, and I'm so angry and distressed. He steps closer to me with a smirk on his face. I swallow shuffling back and he laughs at me "relax babe I'm not gonna jump on you, not until you ask me too anyway." and he unties my hands and turns on his heel, and heads up the steps, the light goes off and we are both left there in the dark. Her cries and her sobbing irritate me I can't stand it, I have no care for her not even for myself and I fall into a deep hole, my life unfolding in front of me, I cannot bear it I detest him he's an animal I'm so angry and full of rage for everything he has done to me and I don't want to go on anymore I simply can't.

I feel her pain ….at least I want to. I want to listen, to wrap my arms around her, to tell her she's not alone, that I care, that it will be ok, that the pain will pass, that it gets better but I can't.

She won't shut up and I don't want to tell her it will be okay, I cannot offer her any comfort I'm one of them I tell myself I have just sat there and watched that! and I did nothing, nothing, oh god what have I done? .He has broken me. I try to close my eyes and shut her out but I can't there is no comfort for me or anyone down there in the dark. I want to die to end this pain and torture and the knowledge of what I have become, I'm desperate to be free from this world and I look for something sharp to help me out of the darkness, all the pain and the demons and a complete sense of hopelessness overwhelm me. As luck would have it there was a shard of broken mirror probably not cleared up from a previous destructive episode down there, and at that moment all I could think about was how it would be best if I wasn't here, the world didn't need any more monsters and that's what I had become. A tear rolled down my cheek and I began to cut through the layers of my skin, I didn't feel any pain, like my mind was numb. I thought about everything that had gone wrong in my life and every bad thing that had happened and the abandonment and loss of my family. As the blood spilled from my wrist, my mind raced and I wondered what it would feel like and I was afraid of death. But when you feel like your burning alive, all you can think of is how to put the fire out as quickly as you can.

Reality

I lay there in the dark the blood seeping from my wrist and I longed for the pain to end, i do not have the strength to cut the other wrist, so I try to cut the open wound a little deeper but it's hopeless I can't even get this right. I have reached the ultimate state of burnout and I do not even have the courage to bring it to an end.

The world was crashing down around me and I suddenly feel so small, the insignificance of my existence greatly apparent

66

and I wanted someone to end it for me.

Sadly I did not get what I wished for, I was full of self-pity and disgust when I heard the footsteps down into the cellar and my body being lifted. Steve laid me on the kitchen floor a shocked look on his face I think he was genuinely in a panic, my body was limp and pale, the blood seeping from my wrist.

"Oh god what have you done?" he seemed nervous and upset, he grabbed a tea towel and tied it tightly around my wrist. "I'm so sorry I really am I will make it better I promise" his voice panicky as he picked me up and sat me in the front seat of his car.

I don't remember getting to the hospital just fleeting flash-backs of bright lights the clanking of a hospital trolley, the sterile smell, and a voice saying please don't leave me.

Everything was hazy was I dead? was it all a bad nightmare I had woken from? I looked down at my arm my wrist was bandaged, I was laying in a hospital bed. Why did he save me I wanted to die, I curled up and began to cry. How would I face everyone? Now was definitely a good time to be anyone but me.

The nurse came to my bedside to check my ops "Can I go home now?" I asked.

"We need the mental health team to speak to you first, and someone will need to collect you, we can't just let you go it's a big thing that you have done." the nurse replied in a condescending manner.

"But I'm ok my boyfriend can come and pick me up if you call him," I said desperately

She perched on the edge of my bed and took hold of my hand." whatever it is you can talk to me, I'm sure I will understand" she was trying to be comforting.

"You can't help me, no one can" I replied sharply "please can you call my boyfriend"

The nurse nodded, "I will go get him he's just gone to get a coffee, he hasn't left your bedside since you came in, he's been really worried about you"

"Oh really" I was surprised by this although part of me knew he wouldn't want me talking to anyone in case I told them what really happened.

A few moments later the nurse came back with Steve following her I could see them talking about me as they walked towards my bed "now we really need to get the psychiatric nurse to see her first and then by all means you can take her home if that's what she wants" she was saying to him in an informing manner, Steve was nodding in agreement and playing the part of the caring doting boyfriend. I played my part too and gushed over him as he came to hug me. "I'm so glad your okay you had me really worried for a moment there" he sounded genuinely concerned for my wellbeing but I knew it was just an act.

The nurse turned to me "you got a good one there, but I recommend you speak to someone, there's obviously something that's brought you to this, anyway the psychiatric team will keep in contact with you, I will go get those discharge papers ready for you" and she smiled.

I so wanted to say something but I knew it was no good and Steve was making eye contact with me saying don't you fucking dare!.

I got dressed and we walked out towards the carpark. I remained silent wondering what the next move would be. We drove off out of the hospital car park. He was silent too and was trying to read his thoughts, I felt uneasy and was not sure where he was going to take me, and a lump came in my throat.

A few miles later he stopped the car, and turned his face to look at me it was a look of pure rage. His fist connected with the right side of my jaw, the left side of my head hit the passenger window and I heard a loud crack. I was dumbstruck but he wasn't finished, he grabbed my hair and pinched my arm, bruising it instantly, then reached over and squeezed my throat.

"Get out!" he screamed at me. I just sat there in shock the tears stinging my eyes. It was late, I got out of the car, numb and overwhelmingly ashamed, and walked a mile to the girl's house as he sped away from me.

On that long walk home I had made up my mind I had to leave somehow I would escape this torment, I did not yet know how but at least I had finally woken up to what he was.

Harriet

Harriet was the first woman I ever had sex with. She was beautiful her dark hair like raven fell to her waist. She had the most amazing green eyes and full lips. She was striking to look at, so dark and wild. Her breasts were creamy white like strawberries and cream. I was attracted to her the moment I saw her and could sense her when she was near me and smell her sweet perfume.

I couldn't sleep one night and crept into her bed. She spooned up to me and caressed my back. I felt so comforted by her. She really was so beautiful and I think she knew that I thought so. She often caught me looking at her naked body. It wasn't like I had no experience, I had had sex with men and another girl but as yet had never touched them and they had only touched me.

I once caught Pru and Molly together and stood and watched, my pussy growing wet. Afterward, I pleasured myself thinking about them.

As I lay spooned up to Harriet I felt her breasts pushed up to my back, I reached for her hand and placed it on my own breast. She immediately caressed it and toyed with my nipple. I felt so horny her touch was unlike that of a man's and I could feel my pussy growing wet. I turned to face her and planted a kiss full on her lips, they were soft and tasted like strawberries, she reciprocated and we were soon locked in an embrace our mouths connected our breasts touching. I felt intensely aware of my own body.

She grabbed my buttocks and pulled me closer to her so our pussy's were touching and I let out a moan of pleasure.

"I want you to touch me Harry" my voice urgent with desire. She put her fingers between my legs and felt my wetness. Her finger stroked gently up and down then circling my clitoris. I took one of her breasts to my mouth sucking hard on her nipple, my body moving against her fingers.

Soon we were entangled, our sex rubbing against each other until we climaxed, and then I lay there in her arms kissing her a feeling of complete understanding of our connection and I knew I loved her.

She was my go-to in my hour of need, someone to feel comforted by, someone with who I could be myself. Some Days I could spend hours in bed with her exploring her body until I knew every curve. Her smell and taste were like nectar to a bee and I longed to stay in this ecstasy forever.

Harry became the second person I had ever loved I adored her and being with her made me feel lighter, happier lost in a fantasy world that I did not want to leave. She was intense to be with and sort every opportunity to fuck me, with no care for time or place and this thrilled me, but Steve was having none of it, he took everything from me including her.

It was a cold dark morning in November I will never forget. Harry had not been seen for a week and although this was not unusual for her she often absconded for a day or two but usually returned when the money ran out. But all attempts to locate her had been exhausted by Eddie and Steve. I had an uneasy feeling from the outset, something wasn't right. Harry had been elusive for some time, she didn't seem present even during our lovemaking. I quizzed her on many occasions but she always shut me down saying she was tired, that she wanted out of all of this, or I was too young and naive to understand. "You have him" she would shout at me. "He fucking adores you!" But I saw how it was with Clara, mother of his child and the jealousy inside me would turn to rage. We would end up shouting at each other, I would cry and beg her not to leave me and she would promise to stay and we would dream up plans of leaving this life and starting out together.

Everything in our house had come to a standstill no one was working and Steve and Eddie spent hours trawling around clubs, bars, and flats looking for Harry. The mood was hostile I didn't dare even look at Steve for fear of a further beating. Clearly, it was all my fault that she had gone missing and the assumption was that I knew where she was. The truth is I was devastated I wanted to find her as much as he did but for selfish reasons, not because she was a commodity he needed back. I hoped that she was happy and safe but sadly that was not the case.

Most of us girls had issues relating to drugs and alcohol of some description, it was a coping mechanism and an addiction deliberately imposed on us to keep control. Over time the need for a better high became more and more intolerable resulting in the use of harder drugs. Heroin had become Harry's crutch.

I didn't notice it at first as I was too consumed in my own destruction, and turning a blind eye to the realities of life was second nature. During one of our lovemaking sessions, Harry had encouraged me to use and injected me with what I now know was heroin an experience I never wished to revisit. At first, I felt fucking amazing and I understood what drove Harry to do it. We were like Gods. I felt like everything was melting and suddenly everything was better. I didn't know that I was capable of feeling that much enjoyment. The initial rush lasted about 20 minutes then there were six to eight hours where I was very relaxed, calm, and had a sense of heightened wellbeing. All my pain and suffering were gone.No wonder she wanted to feel like this all the time. But I wish I could have seen that Harry was dying from the inside out . the years of being trapped in this cycle of sex and abuse had taken her light away.

I awoke the next day feverish and with a strong urge to use again, or maybe that was because the pain I felt needed to be dulled. This was way worse than the feeling after taking speed or cocaine.I felt suicidal, irritated, and unable to relax. My legs really hurt and I couldn't get out of bed. And the stomach pain was unbearable. I was crying curled up in a ball rocking myself. I wanted her to make it go away, Harry couldn't bear it, she felt responsible for encouraging me. Maybe this was the final straw for her. Seeing me in so much pain.

So on that cold dark morning, I knew that life was never going to be the same, that I had lost my beautiful Harry just as I have lost everyone and everything before. And a huge dark cloud bigger than any I had experienced before now was looming over the skies.

Harriet, my beautiful girlfriend the second most important

thing in my life had gone from me forever. She had been found dead in a flat full of squatters, a suspected drug overdose. I saw her lying there in a pool of her own vomit, she was dead she was cold and grey with a vacant look on her face and at that moment I fell apart. Steve picked me up from the floor I screamed hysterically "please don't leave her here!"

but we did leave her there, there was no going back surely this was not who I was, but I had allowed myself to be taken into this lifestyle and this was the true rot and stench of what I had become.

I was hysterical for days following the discovery of Harriet's body. It's so hard to speak when you want to kill yourself. It's above and beyond everything else, and it's not a mental thing it's a physical thing like it's actually hard to open your mouth and let the words come out. They don't seem to be in conjunction with your brain the way normal people's words do, they come out in chunks like an ice dispenser, you stumble on them as they gather behind your lower lip. So you just keep quiet. Steve tried to beat it out of me but losing Harry was the straw that broke the camel's back. I wanted to join her so very much it consumed my every waking thought until eventually, I decided I could not live without her. I was tormented by the picture of her cold body in my head I wanted it gone I wanted to remember her beauty but I couldn't and so I took myself to that dark destructive place I knew well …ly this time I did not reach for the blade but for the pills that had kept me obedient to him and asleep .vodka and 10 lines of coke later and every packet of pills I could find.

I lay in the bathroom lucid drifting off desperate for asleep I would never wake from but oh no that was never going to come I was never to be granted such an easy way out.

The vomiting came with such force I could hardly breathe and wouldn't stop I couldn't tell if I was alive or dead I had pissed myself and lost control of all my bodily functions I was laying in a pool of putrid shit and vomit and I cried out "GOD WHY PLEASE JUST LET ME DIE, AM I SO DESPICABLE THAT NOT EVEN THIS YOU WILL GRANT ME. I AM NOTHING NOTHING I DON'T DESERVE TO LIVE SO WHY "

I can hear Steve's footsteps coming up the stairs. This time it will be different I think to myself.

Steve was stood looking at me with disgust. "You've taken everything from me I am nothing you took my childhood, I've lost my family, you took my beautiful Harry from me it's all your fucking fault I despise you, let me go I beg you please don't take this from me to I deserve this choice at least" I sobbed my voice was desperate, pitiful

Little was I to learn how much worse my life was going to get this was just the tip of the iceberg.

"you wanna die I will beat you to fucking death if that's what you want.do you want me to fuck you with a blade so your pretty pussy bleeds out and you die screaming in pain because I can give that to you !" his voice was hateful and aggressive

"fuck you Eva fuck you this really is beyond what any man can tolerate" and with that, he turned and slammed the door shut.

why was I now left feeling ashamed of myself wanting him to love me so desperately wanting to be everything he desired the torment was unbearable. I feared for my life knowing how angry he was even though hours before I had wanted it to end.

I ran the shower and got in sat crouched underneath the flow of water again trying to wash my shame away and I sobbed for the loss a loss that was so painful I thought it would tear me apart. the physical pain I felt in my side constantly reminding me that I deserved everything that had happened.

Steve was livid he seemed tired of me and the drama I created but he couldn't resist me and the door opened and he climbed into the shower with me and pulled me by my hair "suck my cock bitch" his voice demanding. I did as he commanded thinking I was going to be sick as he pushed himself further into my throat his thrusts hard and brutal with no care and I vomited forcing him to release his grip from my hair. This did not deter him though only encouraged his violent fucking of me as I screamed out in pain. Steve reached an earth-shattering climax gripping my flesh so hard my forearms were instantly bruised my hips redraw and bruises to my inner thighs and buttocks and as quickly as he had entered the bathroom he left.

I know the heartbreak that comes when the shock wears off and you realize that everything has gone. That this is not a bad dream. I'm awake and it sucks. I know the deeper layer of heartbreak when you realize how much pain you are in, how much pain she must have been in, and the weight is crushing.

This time I did not cry though there was nothing.

How i got the scar on my knee

It was a sunny afternoon in June and we had headed out to the countryside for a walk. Steve had packed a picnic so we sat on a blanket and sipped champagne. I relished the time spent with Steve alone, doing things that I assumed most normal couples would be.

It was sticky hot that day I had short denim shorts on and a crop top, my hair twisted into a messy bun leaving curls down the sides of my face and neck. The redness of my hair catching in the sunlight, my blue eyes sparkling naturally my skin glowing in its youthfulness.No need for make up my face was radiant.

laying there with the warmth of the sun on my bare legs I felt happy. We laughed together and talked of our love for each other, my head in his lap as he toyed with my hair, stealing kisses and cuddles on the picnic rug, I wished for the day not to end.

The sun was beginning to set and it had become a little chilly so we decided it was time to head home. I held his hand tightly as we walked back through the woods and when we came to a clearing he stopped and turned to me. I felt a flutter in my stomach but he had that look on his face that said the good times were over. "What?" I asked nervously. Wishing he had just stopped to steal one last private embrace with me.

"I have some friends coming over tonight we will be making another film" he was firm "Please Steve no I don't want to do it, I hate doing those rape films. I don't like them tying me up, they hurt me " my voice a wobble now and a tear falling down my cheek. My legs were shaking at the thought and I felt like I couldn't breathe"You will do it Eva don't disobey me!" he was angry I could see he was not in the mood to argue but it didn't stop me. "I won't do it! I don't want to be hurt anymore please get one of the others to do it" I shouted and released his grip from my hand and started running. I didn't know where I was going and he soon gave chase shouting at me as we ran. The tears falling down my cheeks stinging my eyes made it difficult for me to see where I was going, my heart was pounding, my chest tight so I couldn't catch my breath but I just kept running. It was hard going as the ground was uneven with tree stumps and roots and the brambles tore into my legs but I didn't want the evening events to take place so I kept going. I was so upset that he had spoilt our day by planning this evening's shoot, he always spoilt everything, and I always fell into his trap.

Steve was catching up to me "Eva I will catch you and you will be sorry when I do" I was beginning to get out of breath and as I turned to look behind me I stumble over a tree root and fall cutting my knee. The pain was so bad I couldn't stand and the blood was pouring from a deep gash I tried to get to my feet but knew I would have to admit defeat so I thought maybe I could hide, but Steve's footsteps are getting closer and so I look for a tree to hide behind but as I try to get to my feet his hand is on my ankle dragging me backwards. I scream out as he drags me along the dirt my arms and legs being grazed as he pulled me along. I tremble when his darkness sweeps over me, He stops and pushes my face into the mud straddles me, and starts to pull down my shorts and knickers I am screaming at him to stop but he keeps pushing my face into the mud. "I'm sorry, I'm sorry I didn't mean to run" I cry out. His knee pushes down in the middle of my back with his full body weight, I felt as if he would snap my spine in two, like a twig. At this point, I became intensely focused on him and a strange calmness suddenly displaced my terror as his cock entered my anus "you fucking bitch I'm gonna fuck you till you bleed".he shouted as he grabbed a handful of my hair jerking my head upwards. I clawed away at the dirt with my hands as each thrust pushed harder into me my screams muffled from my face in the dirt.

"don't do this," I said.

Over the next hour, he raped me and tormented me with descriptions of how he would kill me, or telling me he would cut me with his knife. "Or maybe I will just choke you to death," he said pushing my face harder into the mud so I could not breathe. Each time I expected to die, but he always relented just before I lost consciousness.

He slapped me around the head like he was swatting a fly, his cock employed as a bludgeon. What he did to me with it was the least of my worries, those parts of my body that had been reserved as private were no longer mine, and at this moment they were indistinguishable from the rest of my body, also no longer mine.

His rage, a fierce unearthly tempest was what cast me into immense dread.

Time stood still and then it was over.

Eddie

I loved to play games with men it gave me such a thrill especially when I teased them to the point of no return they would be so desperate for me I would suck their cocks until the point of no return then walk away smiling to myself or touch myself in front of them and watch their erection grow I'd rub against them and then chuckle to myself. Id make them beg for it I was such a clever girl so powerful so controlling so tempting.

"I know you want to touch me," I said confidently touching myself provocatively. Eddie tried to avert his gaze but couldn't. we were in the kitchen at Steve's flat two bottles of wine down. Eddie was only there to stop me from leaving so I was using all of my womanhood to coerce him into letting me out for some fun.

His resilience was beginning to break "Eva stop-go put some clothes on you can't just walk round in your underwear in front of me, what would Steve think" "maybe he would think you were fucking me" I laughed. Eddie grabbed me by the wrist "it's not a joke stop laughing about it and put some..."but before he could finish I had kissed him full on the lips my hand on the back of his neck pulling him in my mouth moving to his ear to whisper "you know you want to"he pulled away pushing me back his face embarrassed and angry but I did not give in I stood there and slipped the straps of my bra off my shoulders so that it fell from my breast "what are you doing ?,please Eva just stop" but I could see he was enjoying it ."ok" I said haughtily turning to leave and as I turned Eddie grabbed me and we were kissing each other urgently his hands already pulling my knickers down mine undoing his belt.he lifted me into the worktop grabbed his cock from his fly and penetrated me hard .his thrusts were desperate forcefully he had wanted me for so long and I was enjoying every moment of his unsureness .I goaded him on pushing him to his climax my pleasure coming from the sheer power and control I had right then "Eva please I should stop he was saying"his voice lustful and breathy . but I was not going to let him go I grabbed his buttocks and pushed him hard into me my tongue licking his neck then the ear and then he came and I looked into his eyes and he knew that he wanted me more.

Eddie pulled his boxers and trousers up and went to the bathroom to straighten himself. I stayed on the worktop my knickers discarded on the floor his cum seeping from my wet lips and a smile on my face like the cat that got the cream. I'm so pleased with myself god I love my sexy body I can have anything I want, I can make him do anything I want, and like a light bulb coming on I realized I had accidentally entrapped Eddie but in doing so had started the journey to my freedom from Steve. Eddie was going to be my knight in shining amour he was going to help me escape I would convince him as I had just convinced him to fuck me despite the risks involved for everyone the game was now playing out differently.

Over the next few weeks, Eddie did his utmost to try and avoid me although as my minder this was increasingly difficult and I could see how uncomfortable he was around me. It only spurred me to be more provocative and intimate with him whenever possible the cheeky slap of his arse as I walked by, my hand on his thigh under the table in a restaurant snatching a kiss when alone leading to quick fucks in the toilet of a bar or club or backseat of Eddie's car, I had him in my web he could not escape now there was no going back. Eddie was taking more and more risks sneaking a squeeze of my buttocks or breast when Steve was not looking. He would leave notes down the back seat of the car for me to find and this became our secret way of communication. I wondered if Steve would smell him on me, and the risk of getting caught only led me to pursue him more. but I knew Steve was not suspicious because if he had known I would probably be dead now.

This particular Friday Steve had gone to do some business and instead of Eddie driving him he had left him minding me again. Not an uncommon thing as he couldn't trust me not to abscond or try to take an overdose again. I was so happy and already looking forward to having Eddie to myself all day. He was in the kitchen reading the paper when I strolled past the doorway in my knickers and one of Steve's shirts.

"Hi" I smiled at him twiddling my hair through my fingers ."Come here gorgeous" he smiled back and I walked over and straddled his lap, he was semi-hard already kissing me running his hands up to squeeze my breasts I moaned in sweet delight breathing in the muskiness of him. I unzipped his fly and took out his cock and put it in my mouth my tongue was long and soft and seemed to wrap itself around his hardness. Just as Eddie was about to come, I moved away and began slowly to undress him. I took off his jacket, tie, trousers, shirt, and boxers, and stood in front of him. I took Eddie's hand and brought it under my dress. I was not wearing panties, and his hand felt the warmth of my pussy. It was deep, warm, and very wet. Eddies' fingers were all but sucked inside. ... I stroked his hardness as his fingers probed me. I was about to straddle him when he sat up. "Get up, "he said

Eddie lifted me onto the worktop, I leaned back as he worked his tongue down towards my pussy and began to lick my already wet sex, my legs wrapped around his neck my hips rocking back and forth. after a few minutes, I released my legs and pulled him towards me kissing him on the lips my tongue entwined in his.

"come" I beckoned to him and he carried me to the bedroom. I was really pushing the boundaries now and taking a huge risk inviting him into mine and Steve's bed, but I wanted to be fucked so bad I didn't care. I threw the sheets off the bed and laid back displaying myself to him Eddie climbed on top the tip of his cock just touching me teasing me, I pushed him onto his back and straddled him taking his cock with my hand and pushing down onto his erection. He held me around the waist pushing my hips down on him and then sat up to suckle my nipples our bodies grinding up and down. "Oh Eva god please stop I'm going to come" His voice lustful and breathy. I couldn't help but feel a little smug. His mouth was on mine kissing me as I arched my back and stepped up tempo wanting to release him of his creamy cum, but then I felt it like a wave lapping the sand I didn't want to I did not want to share this vulnerability but I was already lost in the moment and it came like a crescendo I had no control I was moaning and screaming so loud my orgasm igniting the fire in my belly, my mouth biting into his shoulder. This immediately brought him to his climax and we collapsed in a sweaty heap our chests rising and falling our hearts beating fast.

I lay with my head on his chest twiddling the hair in my fingers and a tear rolled down my cheek. I immediately brushed it away not wanting to show my weakness to him I was afraid to look at him my awkwardness making me uncomfortable. I reached into the bedside drawer and took out the pack of cigarettes and lighter slipped on my dressing gown and went to the window to smoke. Eddie came up behind me his hands on my shoulders. "You ok babe?" he questioned . "yeah" I replied taking another drag and then passing it to Eddie, he took a few drags too then went to the bathroom to clean up. I sat back on the bed and fell asleep half naked my dressing gown open my pussy smeared with the evidence of our adventure.

If you play with fire you get burned

This time we had exhausted ourselves. It had been an intense week. My pussy was sore from its many invasions and my breasts ached, my wrists and ankles raw from being bound. Even then I knew I wanted him again that I would soon recover and be glued to him again, I just couldn't stop and my pussy was already twitching.

I laid back and turned and looked into his eyes he smiled and then his face turned angry. "So you have something to tell me?" he questioned me, the fear in my face immediately apparent. What if he knows I'm pregnant I'm not ready to tell him yet.

"I don't know what you're talking about?" I say trying to sound convincing" I'm not going to ask you again ! this is your last chance to tell me" he's angry now and is sat up on the bed his face red the vein on his neck pulsing. "I don't know what you mean" I cry the fear overtaking me.

"You lied to me before when I asked you if something was

going on." his face stern the blood creeping up his neck his veins protruding. "But I haven't lied, nothing's going on" He squeezes my face and looks me directly in the eye. "You're a lying whore" he shouts and pushes my head back on the bed. Opening the bedside drawer he throws some photos at me and punches me in the jaw. I cry in pain and he hits me again harder as I plead him to stop, my hands covering my face.

"What are these ?" I say trying to act dumb, but there they are pictures of me with Eddie on top of me or us fucking in an alleyway. I'm filled with dread knowing the consequences of my dangerous liaisons"You've been following me! I can explain everything. It was nothing it only happened a few times, he took advantage of me I told him no but he wasn't having any of it" my voice quivering in fear.

"Do you think I'm stupid I can see what's going on, it looks like your enjoying yourself !" and he shoves one picture into my face.

"I'm sorry your right, please forgive me, I just got carried away but there's nothing going on" I plead taking his hand "come back to bed" my voice urging him to forget. "I can't trust you can I?" he shouts. And I know what's coming next. He grabs the belt from his jeans and lashes at me twice shouting. "dirty whore" I try to protect myself from the blows but now he is dragging me to the door, the dreaded door I don't want to go through. The tears are stinging my eyes, I sob "please Steve you don't have to put me down there" he looks at me his face full of disgust "I can't trust you, first Harriet and now Eddie! you need to learn some self-control! you need some more lessons in obedience" his voice is hard his eyes glaring at me. I put my hand on the door. "stop please just stop" and I slump to the floor in tears.

"Take me back home I don't want to go into solitary, lock me in my room at home if you must but not down there." my words are shrouded in fear and tears. I look him in the eye looking for the softness I know can be there, I kiss him on the lips in an attempt to persuade him but he pushes me away and storms off to the kitchen. The door remains shut and I sit leaning on it for some time trying to gather my thoughts.

Why does he have to mention her name to me, he knows the pain it causes I fucked her, yes and now she's dead because of me. I can't take this anymore I really do wish I had the courage to walk away but I love him so desperately. I need him just to make me feel alive it's so twisted and wrong like poison. Why am I feeling sorry for myself I deserve no better I knew it was wrong to fuck with Eddie but I did it anyway and I must be stupid to think he would not find out.

I get up and walk to the floor where the belt is lying and take it to him. Steve looks at me and nods I stand against the wall as the lashes of the belt come down on me again and again until I can't stand and my legs buckle under me with the pain but I do not cry.

I could not control myself around him I had started something I knew I shouldn't of. Steve had already called me out and I had promised not to go there again but I couldn't resist. The temptation to break the rules was like a fire burning in me. I felt alive all my senses seemed to be more acute. The more dangerous the more I wanted it the thrill burned in my loins so naturally, I had kept my secret liaisons with Eddie. It had become far more dangerous to pursue this course and much harder to find a time when we could meet, often resulting in a quickie in the backseat as he was escorting me to a job.

This Saturday morning was like every other I awoke in my

bed cold hungry, tired from life. The smell of her was vanishing from my bedding I put my face on her pillow and breathed in but she was gone. My grief was endless and in these moments I felt pain unbearable pain. life went on as usual though. I had been working solidly for 3 weeks doing as I was told like a good girl. Steve was preoccupied with Clara and taking great pride in flaunting their closeness to me. I told myself I didn't care I mean I knew he fucked all of us but I was the special one the girl he adored who he spent endless days with, but at the moment I was furthest from him. Of course, Clara was loving every moment and was rubbing my face in it she constantly flaunted all the gifts he had given her and how they had gone to dinner or to the theatre, and obviously, she wasn't doing any work. Clara had the one thing I didn't, her daughter Rachel, she was one year old and Steve was her father. I resented this so much and couldn't understand why she was allowed to keep her. How had she convinced him? I wondered to myself. It tore me apart, I would curl up in a fetal position racked in agony at the sound of them fucking, wishing it would be me he was with I'd watch them through the open door, the agony burning my soul, but as for Rachel, I loved her as if she was my own.

I did not have time for her I was so grieved and so Eddie helped me to feel some happiness.

At 12:30 Eddie picked me up as usual Steve had asked to see me and I had spent hours doing my hair picking out lingerie and an outfit, I so wanted him to have missed me and so I had chosen a backless dress with a plunging neckline that showed off my figure the swell of my breasts just visible. I really hoped it would turn his head but I expected he would probably just rip it from me, but that's really what I wanted.

Eddie beeped the horn of the car twice I took a last look at myself in the hallway mirror and went out to the car. Eddie stood there holding the car door open and as I got in he smiled."Hi gorgeous "I smiled back at him and watched as he looked me up and down, I guessed I had probably made his prick hard.

I did not speak to him on the ride there but occasionally glanced in the rearview mirror to see if he was looking at me and he was. I enjoyed knowing that he wanted me but he would have to wait all I really wanted was Steve I longed for him to touch me, god, how I missed him.

We pulled up and Eddie opened the car door for me .you may think that this was very chivalrous of him but it was actually because the car doors were locked on the inside mainly to stop us, girls, from running off.

Eddie took my bag and we walked up the steps to the flat. I was expecting Steve to answer but Eddie took the key from his pocket and unlocked the door."I thought Steve would be here ?"I asked confused

"Yeah he said sorry he had something to do and would be back later I was just to collect you at the usual time and wait till he comes back" his voice matter of fact." oh ok," I said stepping into the front room. All the blinds were closed and it smelt of whiskey and stale cigars so I went to the window and pulled the blinds and let some air in. Eddie had followed behind and was soon standing close to me his hand touched the length of my hair and a shiver ran up my spine I mustn't but I want too and before I realize it Eddie has untied the strap around my neck and my dress falls away from my breasts.I'm seduced by the sweet scent of destruction I sigh in anticipation of his touch his hands stroke my bare back and I tilt my neck back

91

waiting for his kiss. his hands are on my breast his mouth kissing my neck it's all too much ." stop Eddie we can't it's too risky"

"I want you now Eva I've been waiting so long and here you are in front of me in that ….god that dress I'm so hard for you," he says squeezing my breast and I give in to him I turn and embrace him kissing him with an urgency he slips my dress down and I step out my body naked apart from a thong .he kisses my breasts and then my belly I'm in ecstasy thinking of him entering me with his hard cock and I want him. I undo his belt and unfasten his trousers and reach in for his hardness stroking it .after a while he discards his clothes and picks me up I straddle him around the waist and he walks me to the armchair kissing me

"oh god, Eva I want you now " his voice breathy "I want you too " I know this is a huge risk doing this here in his flat but I'm so horny I can't think straight. Eddie sits in the armchair I'm on top of him my pussy rubbing on his cock my pleasure mounting and his too I know he wants to fuck me and so I guide his cock in and he starts pumping away harder and faster I'm rocking up and down on his huge member. we are locked together fucking each other like our lives depend on it the world around us non-existent.it's no wonder we did not hear him entered the room I was too consumed in my own pleasure so when he grabbed me by the hair yanking me off Eddie's lap I was utterly shocked and startled. oh, shit written all over my face what came next would live with me forever. Steve punched Eddie square in the jaw knocking a tooth out "I will cut your cock off you Bastard !"I was shouting at him to stop "you stay there you fucking whore I will deal with you later!" he continued to punch Eddie in the face over and over till blood was spitting from his nose and mouth."Please stop you going to kill him" I shout and jumped up on his back trying to pull him off but it's no use he kicks me in the face knocking me halfway across the room, I think he's knocked me out he has broken my cheekbone I later find out. I stay cowered in the corner watching him as he pounds his fists into Eddie. Eventually, I hear a mumble from Eddie and Steve stops hitting him .he looks very badly injured so I try to go to him but Steve grabs me again by the throat . "leave him he's done you will never see him again !"Steve shoves me away and throws Eddies' clothes at him. "Get the fuck out we are done !" he shouts at him pointing towards the door. I look at Eddie and mouth I'm sorry at him but he does not look back and the tears begin to well up in my eyes. The door slams shut and Steve stands there looming over me.

As my mother always said if you play with fire you will get burned.

"So what punishment do you deserve Eva? come on tell me what level of pain you deserve for this!" he is glaring at me and I'm naked and vulnerable. "I iii" stutter back my face in pain."Who do you belong to?" and Steve grabs my foot turning my ankle towards me so I can see his mark carved into my flesh. " I belong to you" I snivel looking at the branding that will never leave me. I point to the cellar door and start to cry uncontrollably ."What's the point Eva I put you in there and what? No, I need to punish you another way."Steve please what are you going to do to me ?"I'm trembling I have no idea what he is going to do. He walks towards me I shuffle back in fear waiting for the first strike, but he takes my face in his hands and looks into my eyes I feel like he is piercing my soul. His thumb rubs across my lips roughly. He takes a small pocket knife out of his pocket and draws down my cheek with the point. I wince with pain "Please don't" He continues to trace the knife down my neck hesitating for a moment "I'm not going to mark your face don't worry you would be worthless to me" and he laughs to himself. He traces down to my breasts pushing the knifepoint against them, I wait for him to cut me but he doesn't. I can't bear it I just want him to get it over with. "Just do it !" I scream at him, but he continues to toy with me.

The knife tip is now at my belly he pushes it hard so it almost pierces my skin and I long for him to push it in. But no he continues towards my pussy, and with the thought of what he might do, I grab his hand and try to guide him up towards my breast. "Don't do it, please cut me here Steve I beg you" He laughs loudly "I'm not going to cut you I'm just playing "

I burst into tears with relief my body un tenses ."Stand up "Steve commands me. I get to my feet and go to pick up my knickers from the floor, he shoves my face down into the armchair. "Smell that, can you smell your disgusting juice on there "He lets go and I gather my knickers up and go to get showered wondering when and how he will punish me, and as i walk he sticks his leg out and trips me over laughing at me. "On your hands and knees like a filthy dog" he commands and I do as he asks crying with humiliation.

I want to see daylight

So I have been sent to a walkup, after yet another huge fight leading to me hitting him in the jaw with my shoe. You see I had started to exert my pain and anger towards him and was lashing out more often, I wasn't afraid to hit back as I knew he would hurt me anyway.

He had broken two of my fingers, fractured a rib, and broken my arm. I probably have had concussion several times I was bruised and battered on my chest, sides, and legs, my upper arms, and throat showing the distant signs of his handprints my wrists often red raw from being bound. I was swollen and sore even bleeding from brute force or foreign objects. My back and buttocks bore the marks of frequent lashings with a belt or telephone cable, but I kept coming back for more. I loved him, needed him like I thought I would die without him! More likely I was going to die because of him.

I was addicted to cocaine and drank heavily and he was self-medicating me with valium

so after another coke-fueled night I had taken offense to his accusations over me screwing other men to make my own money and hit him hard in the face with the heel of my shoe. And now here I am stuck in a walkup for a week, and I don't think I will survive it.

I sit on the end of the bed in this dingy room, my maid waiting for the knock on the door of a client that will be my tenth and it's only 8 pm. I have a small bathroom to clean myself between clients and that's all. They are the dregs of society and have no care for you at all fucking you in every hole their putrid cum seeping from every orifice their grubby hands touching your bare flesh.

I lie there wishing to die, how can I endure this. The breath on my face as they heavy breathe on me I'm so suffocated, the stench of sex unwashable from my body. I cry to myself and they don't even notice just leave their cash and go.

After a while, you feel that you're not even human anymore

just a machine having sex with people, and I really believe I could actually die from it.

I was in an eternal hell, he was punishing me for sure and I want to go back home to him because that's better than where I am now.

The two of us

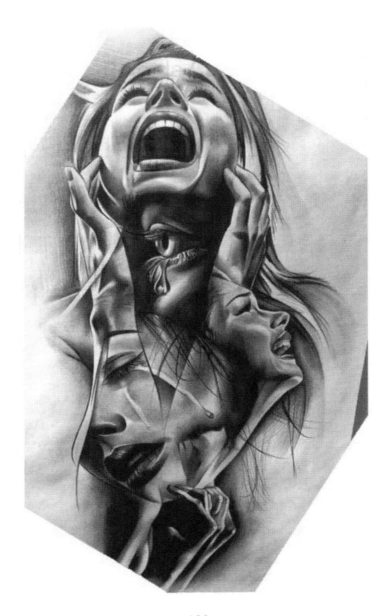

She's here always constantly asking me to stop, to put an end to the pain and torment we feel. Her voice is small but I can hear her I hear him too but his voice is loud and frightening.

She asks me why I don't stop, why I love him, what it's all for but I answer her back with the voice I have become, one of destruction and pain, the one who is in control and wants to play games. She is strong and powerful, she does not need to be caged or chastised, she controls her body, her desires for the dangerous path she walks, her need for the pleasures she seeks that are so dark.

The quiet voice does not like the dark it strangles her and fills her with fear, but I love the dark and want to play there for all eternity. The torment she feels ignites the fuel in her fire. She is a danger to herself and those around her. Where she travels she leaves a trail of broken hearts behind, but she tells herself she does not care for such things and is content to be the wild and exciting woman that she is.

I tell her to take a breath, to be calm, to enjoy the love that she is being shown. I beg her to stop hurting herself as I watch her fill her body with narcotics, as she slices through her flesh again and again, as I watch them fuck her and abuse her. I tell her that her pleasure is short-lived that she will feel the pain deeper afterward, that she will cry in her tormented stupor, that the pain will lead to the opening of wounds that cannot be healed.

She will destroy herself and in doing so will destroy me.

She is so badly wounded, her body cannot withstand the brutality. She cannot mend herself again and again . She is choking me trying to suffocate me,but her attempts to stop me are in vain. I fight back with the last breath in my body, I scream with the last sound in my voice SAVE ME! She does not listen, she cannot be told, her ears are deaf to my begging of her to break free. I tell her I want to be chained, to be locked in the dark where my mind conjures up the evil lurking in the shadows. I'm not afraid I am comforted by it , by the familiarity of my pain.I laugh hauntingly at my weaker self , PLEASE STOP.

She wants to be my friend but my voice is getting quieter now and the bellowing of something else resides, telling her to keep going on this path, telling her she's no good and that the bad is what she deserves. I try to speak up but she cannot hear my soft words, I am being choked by his loudness his control is too strong for me to break.I'm lost in his confusion and disorientation.

She calls to me with realisation , but her mind is lost to the dark to the ferocious beast, she cries in her torment.

And now she is quiet and I can talk to her reassure her, she hears my quiet voice and longs to pull me close, but the chains bound her. In the quiet she is killing us, the two of us will be no more.

I held you to my chest

This was the third day in a row I had woken up and vomited was it the wave of morning sickness or the fear of him knowing that had me retching.

For the second time in a year, I found myself pregnant and I knew it would not end well at fifteen my body just couldn't take this amount of stress on it I was nowhere near healthy enough or old enough to endure a pregnancy after the premature termination of my own doing I feared I did not have the strength to do it again. I wiped my mouth and took a handful of water from the sink and drank it in, flushing the toilet and spraying perfume to disguise the smell I shut the door and clambered back into bed. Now would be a good time to stay with the girls at our house but I had already packed a bag and Steve was picking me up at 12:30.

Eddie pulled up outside just after 12:30 and tooted the horn. I grabbed my bag gave Harry a kiss goodbye and said I'd be back in a few days. As I walked towards the passenger door of the car Eddie got out and opened it for me. "Thanks," I said and got in. There was Steve sat in the back seat I leaned towards him and kissed him on the cheek. "So what's the plan for today" I questioned. Steve just looked at me, and the disappointment was written all over my face. "I thought we could just go to mine and spend some time together, I have missed you, Eva"

"Well if I wasn't working so much" I retorted

"Why do you complain, I'm tired of going over this again, it's your job got it! your not my girlfriend Eva, you're my whore!" his voice harsh

Great I've pissed him off already."don't say that please you know it's not true, I love you and you love me." I stop for a moment telling myself not to push the conversation. "I thought I was special to you, that's what you said, not like the others" a lump appearing in my throat.

"Shut up! just shut up why do you have to spoil everything, shall I just get Eddie to take you back home!" he's shouting now and Eddie glances at me in the rearview mirror as if to say don't piss him off I don't want him to hurt you. So I sit back for the rest of the car journey and say nothing.

We pull up outside the flat and Eddie opens the car door to let me out he grabs my wrist as we turn to enter the house ."Eva I can't stand this any longer, I can't bear him touching you, or anyone for that matter" he whispers so Steve cannot hear us

"Stop just stop I'm with Steve and that's the end of it," I say curtly and head inside with Steve. As we walk through to the lounge Steve stops me. "Don't spoil things lets just have a nice few days together "

"ok" I reply and dump my bag on the couch. His hands immediately round my waist kissing the back of my neck.

"Not now I'm hungry," I say moving away clearly not in the mood for sex right now. But he's already pulling my trousers and knickers down and before I can react he has penetrated me. I let out a small scream as he forces himself in but I say nothing. He fucks me hard and aggressively ripping my bra from my breast and pushing my face into the back of the sofa with his hand, and as quickly as he started he finishes. I gather myself together and storm off to go and shower. As the water runs on my naked body I sob to myself. looking down at the swell in my belly I know that my secret cannot be hidden much longer, and a wave-like feeling of my body being twisted inside out comes over me. I immediately feel sick and start retching my head throbbing. "You better not be sick" I hear him shout and his footsteps coming towards the bathroom door. Luckily I had remembered to lock it. "I'm ok" I shout back, "must be something I ate".His fist knocks on the door and the handle turns up and down. "why have you locked the door, Eva open it at once!" he is pissed at me and starts banging on the door and rattling the handle

"open up!"

I flush the toilet and wrap a towel around me "Just give me a moment" and I unlock the door and he almost falls into the bathroom his face red the vein in his neck popping out. He raises a hand and I step back. "calm down I was having a wee for fucks sake, can't I have any privacy?" I look at him crossly hoping he will see how silly he is .his mouth turns upwards and a half-smile creeps on his face he grabs me by the towel and pulls me to him and wraps his arms around me planting a kiss on my forehead. I squeeze him back and kiss him on the lips. "I won't lock the door again ok" I reassure him. "ok" he replies. Steve pulls me to him again and we kiss our tongues locking together, I bite his bottom lip, my hand caressing the back of his neck and the towel slips from me leaving me naked. I kiss his neck and he kisses my breasts circling his tongue around each nipple as I let out a little sigh of pleasure. He continues kissing and tracing my body with his tongue down to my belly button. I'm enjoying his attention, but my mind is already worrying about him being too close to me. Will he notice my swollen belly?, how can I distract him? His mouth is now kissing my belly and I pray he moves lower down and does not pay too much attention to it. I moan a little louder in an attempt to spur him to lick my pussy telling him I want him there and he reciprocates. After a few minutes of his tongue licking at my wet folds and circling my clit I tell him I want to suck his cock.He stops and I kneel down and take him into my mouth, all the time distracting him from the growing belly I am so desperate to hide.

He tells me to stop and let him fuck me so we move into the bedroom, I lie back on the bed my belly clearly visible to me fear filling me inside as he lies on top of me and I try not to show my discomfort. After five or ten minutes of penetration, he stops and heads back down between my legs with his tongue his hand playing with my left breast and I cannot control my pleasure, my climax approaches so fast my legs shuddering as his tongue continues to stroke me. He moves upwards towards my face and jerks himself off his hot sticky load hitting me. I get up to get some tissues to wipe my face and as I turn to the side he grabs my hand, I can already tell that he has noticed the extra weight I bear and my body stiffens up in an automatic response. I try to jerk my hand from his but he has yanked on it so hard I have fallen back onto the bed, displaying my nakedness my face smeared with cum.I see the redness of his face and that vein in his neck that pops out when he's angry and I've tensed up already in anticipation. He just screams some terrifying noise from deep within and I'm already assuming position to protect myself. "How many times do I have to say I don't want a baby!, you have to get rid of it, do you hear me!" he shouts in my face .im shaking with fear as I know it's too late to get rid of it. "I I I can't get rid of it I'm sorry it's too late please don't be angry" I sputter at him. His fist comes hard on my cheek and I scream out and try to protect my face with my arms. The next punch goes straight to my left ribs knocking the wind out of me and then the next straight to my stomach. Blow after blow comes I gasp with the pain and scream at him to stop but he doesn't hear and the red mist of anger takes over. I think I'm going to die if he doesn't stop soon my attempts to protect myself hopeless. I cry out to him again to stop "the baby please stop" He's hit me so hard I start to vomit.

" I don't want your dirty drug-dependent bastard baby, there will be no baby there is no baby, look at you you wanna get fat and ugly so no one will want to fuck you, now go and clean yourself up then you better get this sorted!"

I say nothing just lie there holding myself my stomach is hurting so badly and I'm sobbing. "shut up with that crying as well god sake you know the rules" and he walks to the kitchen and slams the door shut. I hear him shouting to himself and then the radio come on he does this so he can't hear me crying.

I lay there clutching at my belly and crying uncontrollably it hurts so bad I can't move. My head is spinning and I don't know what to do. I'm laying there the dried cum on my face now mixed with my tears, I tell myself I must get up and get Eddie to drive me home the girls will know what to do. I gingerly stand and stagger to the bathroom and as I walk a sharp pain rips through my belly. I know this pain I've felt it before but this time it's so much more intense. Please don't let this happen I tell myself but it is. The next pain comes a few minutes later and I catch hold of the sink as the contraction waves over me. I catch my breath and then another one comes I cry out with the pain from it ."Jesus where the fuck is he ! I can't do this" but i can still hear the loud music blaring from the kitchen. 3 minutes maybe later the next comes and I've never felt pain like this before I scream out his name "Steve" but he doesn't hear me. Clutching at my belly I try to walk holding onto the furniture as each contraction comes and screaming with agony "Steve please help!" and he hears me this time and opens the kitchen door the music from the radio still blaring out.I look at him my face pleading for him to help me. "The baby is coming" I cry as another contraction starts and then a gush of water. He grabs some towels and tries to help me back to the bathroom. I'm so scared I'm crying "what's happening is it coming out" I cry. "yes Eva it will be over soon" I feel something with the next contraction and bear down my body naturally seems to know what to do. There's a lot of blood and the pain is unbearable I'm screaming so loud. I crouch down with the pain and push the noise from me so guttural as I push and Steve takes the baby and wraps it in a towel. It's a girl. I'm crying uncontrollably I already know the outcome ."let me have her, Steve please I want to hold her "I'm shaking uncontrollably with shock. "Its dead Eva" his voice flat. "Don't say that, let me see her" I'm begging him. He grunts at me with that annoying look and hands the towel to me. My baby is lifeless her skin thin like tracing paper, she's the size of a bag of sugar. I look at her so complete with all her fingers and toes. My walling so guttural as I hold her to my chest and rock back and forth.

"Eva come on give it to me" he demands but I won't let go of her I continue my walling so he leaves me for a while. I'm exhausted now it feels like hours have passed and I'm still there holding her. I know I have to let her go but the loss is ripping me in two and I wish Harry was here.

The door opens and Steve sits beside me a pair of scissors in his hand. "Give it to me Eva" I hand her to him and he lays her on the bathroom floor and cuts the cord away. He wraps her back in the towel and goes to leave I cry out "where are you taking her ?" I scream at him.

He gives her back bundled in the towel. The afterbirth comes next and I cry with the pain as I hold my dead baby in my arms. I won't recover from this I definitely do not have the strength to continue anymore. I am consumed with grief Steve beating me, again and again, will not make me subservient to him, something inside me is fighting to break free but right now I want death and all its darkness and fires of the burning pit of hell. I feel it deep inside me.

I need medical attention but it's not an option so I hold her to me until late into the evening, she is cold and grey and I know I have to let her go. I shout for Steve to come to me. He walks into the bathroom and takes her from me and places her on our bed. I get into the shower my place of rebirth and let the water wash over me, I don't think it possible to cry this much but it is.

Later when I have dressed and tied my hair back I lay next to her on our bed sipping hot tea the crying coming in intervals. I place my tea on the bedside table and pick up the bundle and walk to the kitchen where Steve is sitting. It's hard to speak but i do ."What are you going to do with her?" I question him."

109

Come," he says his voice soft and gentle.

I give her to him and we take her to the garden."Now listen to me Eva you know this was going to happen, someone like you can't have a child you understand? don't you"

And I do understand. There's a hole already dug deep enough for her and Steve places her in there and covers her over with the loose soil.I cannot control my grief and desperately try to claw the soil away and uncover her my distress taking on a life of its own like some creature from the darkness.

There is beauty in this beast

There must have been something about me that gave me away. maybe it was the way I looked up to him and admired his cocky confidence. I was drawn in by the attention he gave me, the way he looked at me. How does a young child understand how wrong it is when it seems to answer all the questions. Someone has noticed me and finally, I'm not alone. Nothing else matters. It doesn't matter that now I have an unspeakable secret that must be kept from my parents, it doesn't matter that the shame I feel when I am around people has caused me to hide inside myself, it doesn't matter that I can't bear to be looked at because I'm so scared that I'll be found out and exposed. At least somebody loved me, right?

I'm not sure who I really am? this question never leaves me, he molded me into the girl that stands before you. Yes, a woman I am in body, but a girl still in my mind.

This girl is full of love but not the kind in fairy tales oh no the kind that is dangerous that destroys. It's overwhelming and filled with fear. It's a love she does not make sense of, it's an ideal a concept something her heart desires beyond anything or anyone else. It burns so fiercely inside of her that it becomes out of control sending flickers of flames through her burning those around her. She does not want to cause them harm but the overpowering need in her ignites the flames so they scorch her insides and in turn, she releases them in a torment of pain and grief.

He has succeeded in this creation of her, controlling her very existence for she cannot extinguish or dampen the flames for if she carries this out leads to her body shutting down provoking illness so grave that the only way to halt her demise is to relight the fire, only now it burns fiercer than ever and glows madly through her eyes her salty tears offer her nothing.

She begs him not to stoke those smoldering embers or add more firewood but he revels in her anguish offering her some solace with the promise of lesser firewood if she surrenders herself to him.

This girl is like a red hot ember that cannot be touched by those that could love her, but only to be touched by him for he is resistant to her heat. There is but one thing that her fire provides and that is her enchantment. So you see if the fire burns out so too will the enchantress and that's all this girl has.

"People only love you as long as they're getting something of you, but the minute you say something they don't want to hear or do something they don't want to see, all the admiration drains from their hearts."

112

Rewind

I suppose I really ought to explain how I ended up in this predicament in the first place.

My parents would tell you I was a difficult child always getting into one scrape or another. I knew I was the bad sheep of the family, my mother certainly made sure I knew that, and would constantly blame me for things and put me down. She said nothing was ever enough for me that I always wanted more, and on that, she was right for sure.

I was curious about my sexuality and my body from around the age of ten, up to this point I had no knowledge of the adult world or what was happening to my body, and when that fateful day came and I saw the blood was in my knickers I thought I was dying, it was utterly terrifying, and this seemed to annoy my mother even more. She was now forced to explain to me and my sister who was three years my senior about periods and the birds and the bees, something she seemed to be uneasy with.

But as I grew accustomed to the monthly visits I also felt my body changing and embraced it. I began to notice that boys looked at me and that if I held myself in a particular way they would get embarrassed. I was starting to feel different adolescence were creating a hormone storm in my body like something was trying to break free. I was the coolest girl for a while. I would plait my hair tight at night so in the morning it would fall down my back in ringlets. At the age of eleven, I had kissed various boys and shown several of them what lay beneath my knickers, I found it exciting and before long became the attention of most of the boys in my school especially some of the older ones. Inside somewhere I had a feeling that what I was doing was wrong or forbidden but all that did was excite me more. I became more and more provocative and longed for the older boys to touch me, I didn't care who they were I wanted them to feel my pussy and bring me to orgasm as I rubbed their little cocks. sooner or later I was wanting more and would lie there with a look that said please take my virginity, but none of them would much to my annoyance and I thought to myself they were too immature and I needed a man.

You could say that I was popular in school and that people use to flock around me but I only really had a couple of true friends, most of the others just talked about me and my outrageous behavior and I didn't really care I was having so much fun.

So how did a thirteen-year-old girl from a small town become the victim of a sex trafficking ring?

Well, I realize now that the shock of my father leaving that year out of the blue two weeks before Christmas was probably the catalyst, but I was already on the wrong path so this was probably the nudge that took me down that dark course.

114

I really had no idea what effect my father leaving would have on my thirteen-year-old self but it was catastrophic. I spiraled further into trouble often resulting in the police bringing me home for getting blind drunk in a park somewhere. I was vulnerable and I didn't know it but I had been targeted by a man who wanted to exploit me, he promised me something better than I thought I already had, he groomed me like he was my boyfriend, I know that now.

I think back to then and see a desperate young girl craving attention from somewhere and maybe that's why he chose me. So much has happened since that first night when I was finally made a woman and realized there was no going back.

He lay there next to me gently caressing my naked body. I tried to cover myself but he told me I would enjoy it, and to my shock the more he touched me the more I felt the pleasure in my body, I was wet though I hadn't known I would be, I felt ashamed of myself but I touched him back, when he pushed himself inside me it was not the intrusion it had been earlier, but like something that was a part of me. I hadn't any sense of wanting him to finish and pushed myself against him to feel more before I realized I was feeling my orgasm rising, something I had only experienced by myself I wanted to cry out so badly it was so intense I tried to quieten myself but it was no good and soon my squeals of pleasure echoed the room, I felt I was about to burst wide open. It was the strangest sensation, something that went beyond simple sexual pleasure. It felt as if something inside me, something special inside me, was slowly working its way through me, my emotions overwhelmed me and hot tears streamed my face, and there began my lesson in the art of men. He taught me everything, what my body could do for me and what my body could do for him and soon

115

we were fucking and something in me snapped an emotion like no other took over my whole being and I was consumed with need and a wanton desire for him. In three days he had transformed me into this needy sexual being who just wanted to learn more and more and I felt so alive.

The truth is that he had manipulated me into staying I was trapped in a cycle of physical, emotional, and sexual abuse, but I utterly adored him and did not yet know what lay ahead for me, initiation! (.we will come back to this later)

Within a few months of being with him, he had convinced me that my family didn't want me and I was using drugs and within a month he was prostituting me

It was glamorous for a while, I had new clothes jewelry and lots of money he was well dressed and always had a group of women around him. It looked like he took care of them and he would get us drugs whenever we wanted. I utterly adored him and was consumed by his attention to me, we would spend whole days fucking with him telling me how beautiful and special I was.

But by the time I was 14 I had been beaten and raped more times than I could count.

Clients paid £80-£100 for half an hour, or £160-£200 for an hour. Some left me bleeding, or unable to stand, or in so much pain that I thought I may die. But there was no going back I thought. He used me to make sex videos or rather rape porn as I see it now, I hated it they were so brutal and left me injured and in pain, but I was the best because I made it look realistic! Well, that's because it was real.

So I joined him into a life of hell. I had sold my soul.

Even though I knew it would make him angry I fought him every step of the way, I think he found this a challenge that he greatly accepted. He had rules that needed to be abided and this was a constant battle of wills between us. I was not allowed out by myself, men were forbidden at the girl's house and I was to obey every command he gave me during intercourse. I didn't want to be naked all the time, but he said it would teach me to be confident in my body. I didn't like his friends touching me or having to perform oral sex for them. I didn't like him tying me up and videoing me I hated the camera as soon as I saw it I knew I would be subjected to sexual violence to be watched by others. And so I would exert my dislike and in turn, this would lead to more violence.

Do Gooders

~~~~~~~~~~

I had an anger inside me it was pure rage at times and I couldn't control my destructive outbursts. At school, I was constantly acting out my feelings and was well known for my behaviour by teachers and heads of year. My parents got constant phone calls regarding my behaviour and concerns over my welfare but no one could seem to understand me. They all tried to no avail they didn't have a clue of the trouble I was in. My head of year who was also my science teacher often bore the brunt of my foul mouth and vicious tongue. On this particular occasion, I had taken a dislike to her suggestion that I needed to move to the front of the class and pay more attention. "I'll show you attention you fucking bitch "I screamed and with that launched my stool and threw in her direction. Of course, I was summoned to her office to await my punishment. I sat outside her door waiting for her to summon me inside,I was cocky and arrogant when the door was pushed ajar and her stern voice called me to enter. I just wanted to get it over with so I could sneak a quick smoke in the girl's toilet before my next lesson bell rang. I slumped into the chair opposite her desk making no eye contact. Eva, we need to talk. Boring! My head was telling me to just nod in response to whatever she said and then just as I waited for her words of distaste followed by how bright you are and hour letting yourself down she opened a packet of cigarettes and offered them to me as she lit one herself.I was surprised I mean I knew she smoked but to offer me one. I did not let my shock at her gesture show and took a cigarette from the pack and lit it inhaling deeply on the tobacco taste. No words were said I smoked the whole cigarette and stamped the end out in her already overflowing ashtray and waited patiently for her to speak. Silence she said nothing but had this concerned look on her face. I began to feel uncomfortable and restless and shuffled in the seat. Eventually, I could take no more of this awkwardness "what" I shouted at her my anger welling up inside me "what the fuck, just give me a detention and let me get to my next lesson "

"I'm not going to give you a detention Eva it would be a waste of time you wouldn't even turn up would you?"her voice was direct

"Look I'm sorry for acting up ok that's what you want me to say now can I go" i mumbled

"No Eva you can't go I want you to sit there and think really hard about what you want to tell me" and she proceeded to light another cigarette offering the packet again to me. This was all so confusing I had no idea what it was she wanted me to say and I could feel that I may be stuck there in her office for some time. I bet everyone in class would be talking about me and reckoning I was going to be excluded. I may as well have another cigarette whilst I'm here and anyway it might calm me down a bit. I reached forward to the open pack and in doing so the sleeve of my shirt rode up my forearm revealing some large bruises and rope burns on my wrist I immediately yanked my sleeve back down to cover it and lit my cigarette. she just sat and watched me whilst I took a long drag she was waiting for something. I wriggled uncomfortably in my seat the awkwardness of the situation making me angry."I'm fucking leaving ok bitch and there's nothing you can do about it" I shouted as I stood up and grabbed my bag flinging it over my shoulder. I stepped forward to put out my cigarette and headed for the door but she was up and standing in front of it. "Fuck off I want to leave " I screamed my anger now turning to tears that I'm trying not to cry "please can I just go, I don't want to do this right now I have nothing to say "and a tear escapes and rolls down my flushed cheek.

"I think you do have something to say Eva I think you have a lot to say and I'd like to hear it" she's calm just standing there. I make one last ditched attempt to escape her office and barge into her "move just fucking move!" she grabs my arm and pushes me back "stop!" she shouts back at me, I try to move forward but she's blocking me and my rage has now turned into crying and I just can't fight so I sit back down a hot mess of tears on my face.

"I'm a fucking idiot " I cry and she hands me a tissue."I'm in so much trouble I can't "I stutter " you wouldn't understand you just wouldn't "

"Try me I'm sure it's not all that bad really whatever it is I can help" her voice is reassuring

" But you can't help you see no one can," I said slamming my fists onto her desk.

"Look Eva I'm not as stupid as you would like to believe and I can see that your hurt,

120

I've seen the bruises,hickies,I have noticed when you seem to be in pain or discomfort. Half the time you look like you just got out of bed, I'm not sure if you have even been home or slept in the last week, now please talk to me, I can help you ." she sounded genuinely concerned but also firm.

"I really can't tell you anything I'm fine honestly I'm just tired" I wasn't going to talk to her she would surely call the police or something and if my parents get any more phone calls well I really don't know what will happen.

A part of me wanted to just blurt it all out the misery of it all and I was just wanting someone to hold me.

"I'm not buying any of this "she grabs my shirt and pulls my sleeve up."This isn't normal Eva someone has hurt you and I need you to tell me who."

"DONT FUCKING TOUCH ME!!!!"I grab my arm back and go into self destruct mode grabbing everything I can and throwing it around the room papers scatter across the floor ashtray and dirty cigarette butts, my bag hits the door making a loud thud "ARGHHHHH!!!"I'm vocalising my anguish loudly not even aware of my surroundings until I feel exhausted and as I fall to the floor in a heap she moves towards me and holds me so tightly I can hardly breathe. I stop fighting her and hold her tightly back like I'm holding on to my very existence.

I'm just a blubbering mess and she is soothing me with her shh's and there there's stroking my hair away from my forehead and I feel I could just stay there forever.

The door of the office flings open and another head of year and a teacher from the classroom opposite have heard the commotion.

"Everything ok?" one of them asks her

"Yes yes," she replies ushering them to leave and close the

door behind them.

Oh fuck I'm in trouble now everyone's going to hear about this.I break my hold but she doesn't let go of me so I wriggle till she loosens her grip.

"I'm so sorry honestly miss I didn't mean to wreck your office I guess I will be excluded for sure"

"Eva I'm not concerned about any of this but you do need to talk to me, what was that all about?"

I wipe the tears from my face and the snot from my nose with the back of my sleeve. She hands me a box of tissues

"Ok I will talk but you have to promise I won't get into any trouble, or you won't call the police or tell my parents," I say "Promise me you must promise"

"Eva I'm not going to say anything I'm just here to listen and help if I can but I may have to speak to the authorities if I'm concerned for your welfare"

"How can I trust you? you don't want to help you're just like everyone else trying to control me" I said harshly

"Whos controlling you Eva? please talk to me I am very worried about you is someone making you do things you don't want to do?" she sounded like my mother condescendingly.

"Sex! the word is sex or fuck or whatever I'm not a child so just call it what it is!"I said holding my head in my hands.

"you got any more of those cigarettes I need one I can't think straight"

she offered them to me and I immediately lit the end taking a long drag and then exhaling the smoke, again and again, she too lit a cigarette her face looked pale and lost. She clearly has no idea what I'm about to say. Everyone thinks they can help but it's all too late I'm in far too deep to stop now I love him and it hurts.

122

"Can you tell me what you're being made to do?" she says pausing for me to speak

I could feel myself getting angry but I think it was not anger but just the sheer weight I was carrying it felt like if I spoke I would explode.

"He doesn't make me do anything, you've got it all wrong , it's not like you think I want to be with him,I love him …
..It's just sometimes I make him mad and well anyway there's nothing to say honest there's not, we had a fight that's all, and it's okay now because I will do better next time"the river of words just seemed to flow out into a garbled mess.

"Eva it sounds very frightening to me you, shouldn't feel like this, love is not supposed to cause you harm and I think you are being harmed, I'm right aren't I?" her voice seemed to be pleading with me to let her into my dark world.

"No honest it's not you don't need to worry about me, I'm fine I've just been tired a lot and it makes me irritable and then I just say things I don't mean, I really do need to get to my lesson now miss"I'm pleading now for her to unhear the words I've said adamant that she is wrong.i want her to let me go back to class where I can be the thirteen-year-old school girl that I am, but I can see that she is having none of it as she keeps questioning my answers.

"Ok Eva you have it your way but I'm going to just say it …." she sighs deeply and pauses before the awful words come." I think that whoever this boyfriend is that he is making you do things you don't want to do , I believe that he is prostituting you!" there I've said it

My hands are covering my ears and my hard outer shell is cracking I do not want her to say it because the truth is too painful for me to hear and as the word prostituting leaves her mouth I cry out "NOOOOO! please don't say it I don't want you to say it" and I break down into floods of tears again.

She pulls her chair up next to me and puts her arm across my shoulder to comfort me.

I'm a blubbering mess but telling her the truth feels like a good thing to do . Maybe she could help me because I really don't want to have sex with all these men but at the same time I love Steve and I can't bear to not be with him he is there every waking moment, I can't eat, sleep or concentrate on school, and he's pushing me more and more to spend more time with him.

" He makes me have sex with other people but I'm not a prostitute really I'm not !" my voice an angry whisper."Please you can't tell this to anyone "I'm scared now because deep down I'm afraid of him he frightens me and know how much pain he can inflict on me I believe he would kill me.

"Eva I just want to help, I won't put you in any danger of course but I would like you to think about how I may be able to help you because you know that what he is doing to you is wrong."

"I will think about it but right now your just upsetting me and I can't think straight, you don't have any right to keep me here, your just making things worse coz now everyone will be talking about me!" my voice showing my disdain.

Of course, deep down I wish she could just scoop me up and take me away, just for a while so I can feel what it's like to be loved really loved in a parental way but in truth, she would just end up judging me. Everyone judges, you see and they all think that they have the answers or some sort of magic key that will unlock what's hidden inside me. If only they knew how complicated it really is even if they had a key they would be unlocking the door to a labyrinth, endlessly taking them down the wrong path. I used to wish I had a key, a key that would unlock my parent's love but I never found it. The problem was I couldn't be saved and I don't think anyone was meant to save me I was on exactly the path that I was supposed to be on for some reason this was my destiny.

My path in life had been chosen long before today , maybe even from the night I was born, I just wasn't meant for good things no matter how hard I tried I was just wicked through and through.

I dont know what love is

I'm covered in glass. My head is bleeding. Now I am screaming.
I climb out my passenger-side door and instinctively touch
my face. Blood. How hurt am I? I can't feel anything.

"Eva, you bitch," he says. The metal shovel he broke his
car window with now out of his hands, he follows me inside,
trying to stop me along the way. "Eva!" he shouts. *Get out of
my way.* I must see how hurt I am. I walk into the bathroom
and look in the mirror. There are lines of blood coming down
my face, but I can tell nothing is deep. I'm wearing sunglasses,
which thankfully protected my eyes from the glass that had
just been launched into my face.

"Don't! ignore me !" his feet thundering up the stairs.

I stare at myself blankly in the mirror as I begin to dab at the
blood. My heart is pounding, and I barely recognize myself.
The blood-streaked reflection keeps looking at me, but who is
she? How did I get here? He tries to take over at dabbing the
blood off my face. I tell him to get the fuck away from me, but
he grabs my wrist, and so I let him tend to my cuts.

I was tired of him using his physical size to intimidate me or block me from running away. I had thought locking myself in his car would allow me a small amount of breathing space. How stupid was I? He made me feel so scared and powerless, but he also looked at me in a way I had not experienced before and his touch was electrifying I was consumed by my wanton need for him even for physical violence. You see any form of touch was better than no touch at all.

I sat perched on the edge of the bath, tired from the constant battles with him. But even at this moment, I long for him to hold me as a mother nurtures her child, and before I can think of the pain and anguish I'm in I find myself pulling him close to me kissing him hard on the lips, no words are needed between us he knows instinctively what I desire and in a moment we are entangled in each other's kiss his hands on my breast squeezing it firmly my hands on his buttocks pulling him tightly to me so as I can feel his growing erection. As I pull him closer he pushes himself against me my legs now spread as he stands between them. He's pushing up my top now and pulling down the cup of my bra to reveals my breast his mouth then latches onto my nipple and I moan with pleasure and as I lean back my we fall into the bath and explode into fits of laughter and I have forgotten how angry I was before. We compose ourselves and continue having sex.

He's done it again I'm trapped in this cycle with him I don't know what's love and what's abuse they are intertwined in my soul. I cannot live without him and so I accept that he knows best that only he can know what I need and that dreaming of a better life is futile for the only life I can have is the one with him by my side, in my bed, my thoughts, and dreams, his blood running through my veins and pumping my heart. He is what keeps me living.

You are my worst twisted nightmare, laced by the distorted beauty.

I long to be able to break free to live on my own

leap

"Nobody will save you, so you might as well give up now!" Steve shouted angrily at me as he cuffed my hands to the wall.

"Please don't "I shout back, but he's already removed the belt from his jeans ready to hit me with. "Turn and face the wall" he orders and I oblige after all nothing will stop his course so it's best to get it over with.

He lashes out at me the first strike of the belt hitting me hard across my buttocks making me cry out, and before I have time to catch my breath the second strike comes harder than the first and I cry out again the pain searing through me. The third strike knocks me clean of my feet causing me to be dangling by my wrists. I try to gather myself and get back to my feet but I can't take anymore.

"Stand up!" he screams at me. "Are you deaf? I said stand back up! , do you want me to add another five? you dirty little slut!" I manage a "no" and brace myself for two more strikes. They come in quick succession leaving me in a heap

129

constrained by my wrists which are now red raw. I'm crying uncontrollably as he approaches me looping his belt back into his jeans. He takes hold of my face firmly. "You can't leave me. You couldn't live without me." he spits in my face.

I want to tell him then and there but I'm afraid he may kill me and whereas before I would have welcomed him bringing me to my end, I now want to live.I have a reason to survive I just need to hold out a while longer.

"you hurt me you son of a bitch!" I shout at him and he just laughs and leaves the room.

So far my plan to leave this life is not going at all well, I've tried to run away, I've tried to ask him to let me go, I've shouted in his face and told him I'm leaving it's no use, but I have to leave and not because of all the previous events but because my unborn child's life depends on it. Somewhere within me I still have the strength to do this and I don't have much time my pregnancy will soon give me away and I'm sure he will kill me then. My mind is made up I want to live I want my unborn child to live even though I know it will be painful to do so.

I sit my hands still cuffed to the wall and I pray for some guidance, I actually start to pray out loud. Is God really there? I cannot believe he would let any of this happen to me but then I have wandered so far from the path that I am beyond salvation. I look down at the swell beginning to appear above my pubis the first glimpses of what grows inside me and I cry until I cry myself to sleep. I'm so tired now maybe it's a hopeless cause and I should just give in to the end.

Unaware of how much time passes I stir to see him un cuffing me and in his loving arms he scoops me up and holds me to him. "I'm sorry Vicky, you just make me lose all control of myself and I need you to understand how it is here with me, you know don't you? I can't accept your insolence, why do you have to fight with me, can't we just fuck like we usually do.I love you Vicky you're so special to me" his voice is soft and apologetic and I think to myself maybe he really does love me, but the thought is just a fleeting one. He places me on our bed and strokes my hair and the anger and hurt I felt before evaporates and I turn and kiss him."Vicky my beautiful girl" He kisses me back so I undo his belt and jeans and start to stroke his cock, it hardens within a few moments I straddle him teasing him rubbing myself against him, he pulls me down and kisses me squeezing my breasts and I know he wants me. He flips me onto my back and pushes up my t-shirt to reveal my breasts, his tongue circles my left nipple teasing it with his lips and then trailing down to my belly, I moan in anticipation .he moves down between my thighs, and teases me through my knickers for a while before sliding them down my thighs and discarding them. His lips fastened on my swollen little bud leaving me moaning and writhing. "oh please Steve" I moan desperately for him to lick me, and his tongue licks at my wet opening, my thighs trembling his mouth fastened to my pussy and I cry out as he brings me to climax.

"I'm goin to fuck you now," he says his expression lustful. He presses the tip of his cock at my entrance then with one forward thrust penetrates me. I dig my nails into his buttocks and urge him on unashamedly lost in the pleasure. He throws his head back, his teeth are clenched and his thrusts more frenzied and I begin to feel his climax coming. He pulls his cock almost out and then buries it back in me up to the hilt and I scream out "I want to see you come" and he pulls out his sperm jetting across my belly.

We spend the next few hours consoling each other, after all,

I need him in a better mood than earlier and so I tell him I won't go and that I love him.

Breaking free

" You were just an experiment!" he shouts in my face. "I'm pregnant!" I scream back at him please stop hitting me. "you have to let me go, the toy you wanted is broken, you cannot play with me anymore" my voice is desperate and scared. Surely he will kill me now. I'm sixteen

weeks pregnant and I don't want to die.

He wrestles me to the floor his fists constantly pounding at my back and thighs, anywhere he can get to. I try hard to protect my stomach from his blows.

In a moment he stops, he has heard what I have said "YOUR WHAT!, I don't believe you your a liar" he's angry but has stopped beating me.

I run to the kitchen and grab a knife from the drawer "don't you fucking touch me" I scream at him the blade in my hand my hand shaking.

He laughs at me and I lunge forward at him.

I'm shocked and in disbelief as the blade goes in. I really

have stabbed him, and I know what I'm capable of, I want to stab him again and again, but the sheer shock of what I have done leaves me stunned I just stand there the knife in my hand, the blood on its blade, my hand is shaking and I drop the knife to the floor.

Steve has slumped on the kitchen floor the blood seeping from his side, his shirt already soaked. He puts his hand to his side in disbelief. What have I done?

I lift his shirt to see the wound, it looks deep and I don't know what to do or how to help him, I'm in a panic and try to hold my hand there to stop the bleeding. I'm afraid of what I have done and I'm afraid of losing him. My mind is racing if he dies I will go to prison I'm so out of my depth I have no control over my rage it cannot end like this. I don't want him to die.

"You stabbed me" he shouts in disbelief his bloodied hand squeezing my throat"Shit that hurts, your gonna regret this" his voice is shaky I think he is in shock. "I don't know what to do, tell me what to do I'm so sorry I didn't mean it" I cry in frantic desperation.

I pick up the phone shaking and dial Eddies' number, he will know what to do. Crying and spluttering down the phone "Eddie it's me Eva, oh god what have I done" I can't get my words out. "Calm down Eva what's going on I don't understand you has he hurt you? is it the baby?"Eddie sounds worried but calm. "I stabbed him, I fucking stabbed him and there's blood everywhere, I need your help Eddie please help me I don't know what to do" I'm frantically pacing up and down Steve is clutching at his side moaning.

"Who have you stabbed Eva where are you?"Eddie is calm and precise "Steve I've stabbed Steve, he knows about us, and"

134

and my voice breaks I'm crying uncontrollably.

"I'm coming over now, just keep the pressure on it" Eddie's voice is concerned.

I hang up and tell myself to get a grip. I take a tea towel from the drawer and press it firmly onto the wound. Steve is looking pale and sweaty now and I stroke his forehead comforting him.

"Eddie will be here shortly just hang on he will know what to do, just stay with me, please don't leave me" the fear is obvious in my voice.

Eddie screeches up outside the flat and comes barging in through the door. "Fucking hell Eva!" he shouts at me and pushes me to the side rushing to Steve's aid. "Help me then we need to get him in the car and to the hospital!" I'm so shocked I just stand there looking at them both unable to move. "Eva! for fucks sake! help me" Eddie is shouting at me and so I take hold of one side of Steve and help Eddie lift him to the car.

"You'd better stay here and get the place cleaned up I will sort everything out, don't speak to anyone!" he is firm with his instructions and I nod in agreement.

As I shut the front door I collapse to the floor my head in my hands. I can't leave now, oh god what have I done I will surely die for this. I want him to be ok, will he be ok? I feel a lump in my throat as I realize I have failed again, that I will be stuck there for a while longer and that my life is now in even greater danger.

My hands are sticky now from the blood and there's a pool of it on the kitchen floor, the knife is still where I dropped it and bloody handprints are on the cupboards and floor, I need to get cleaned up. I go to the bathroom to wash my hands and see myself in the mirror, my face now stained in his blood. My heart is in my throat, I can't breathe as I turn the tap and run my hands through the water turning it red. I feel a strong urge to end my life then and there, I cannot get the picture out of my head, the feeling of the knife going in one minute the next I had stabbed him. In a moment of pure rage I am a murderer, what if I have killed him?

In my distress the thoughts spin round in my mind, the police coming to arrest me, the trial, being in prison, my unborn child being born and taken into care, or worst of all given to my mother. It will be better if I die now and my baby never has to be born into this cruel world. But even now in the darkest moment, I do not have the courage. I cannot live with myself I cannot take another life I feel the baby inside me and I know I must preserve this life if its the only good thing I ever do.

The blood-red water washes away down the sink and I splash my face with the cold water and rub the blood off with my hands. I look back at myself in the mirror, my eyes are red from crying my hair tousled across my shoulders, my t-shirt covered in blood.I grab a hair tie from the shelf and scrape my hair back into a ponytail, then discard my t-shirt.

Taking the mop from the kitchen larder I fill the bucket with water and begin to mop the floor, but it just seems to be spreading the blood around so I resort to a cloth and scrub away on my hands and knees. The time seems to tick on and on but eventually, the kitchen shows no remnants of what has passed. I take the rest of my clothes with my t-shirt and put them in the washing machine and press the button. The drum spins round and round filling up with water and I sit and watch my mind in a daze.

How long has it been? I ask myself is he ok ? when will Eddie return?. I need to occupy my time until then. I flick through magazines not really looking at anything, flick through tv channels but nothing can take my mind of the events of this afternoon.

I lay on the sofa and pull a blanket over me and nod off to sleep, my mind taking me to faraway places.

Eddie and I had been planning a way for me to leave for six months now, he promised he would help me but now I was not so sure after all I had just stabbed Steve and he knew Eddie had been fucking me so maybe all hope was now lost.

Eddie had helped me save £3000 in cash that I had creamed of the top of jobs or stolen from Steve's secret stash not so secret as I knew where it was. I was careful only to take small amounts at a time as to not draw attention to the stacks of twenties going down.

I had enough to get me started and Eddie said he had found me a flat back in my home town and I had been speaking to my mother about the baby and she seemed to want to help me. Truth is her head was buried in the sand as usual but I had played her a rather convincing story of how I was going to get a job and bring my child up and never look back and that we could be a family again.

But now it looked like that was never going to happen, I had lost control again and destroyed every chance I had of a normal life.

moving on

Even today years after I got out of my dangerous life with him. I yearn for a freedom I may never have.

The flat was small and basic, but it was safe and it was to be my home. Eddie had furnished it with a few essential items, there was a double bed and chest of drawers in my room and a beautiful pine cot. The second bedroom had a single bed and a fitted wardrobe. Through to the hallway was a small bathroom with a bath toilet and sink and then another door leading to the sitting room. There was a cream carpet that was soft under my toes and a small beige sofa. In the corner was a unit with a TV and at the end was an archway through to a galley kitchen. It had everything I needed I was so happy.

"Thank you, Eddie, thank you so much this is so much more than I expected" I shrieked with joy.

"It's nothing, I'm just glad you like it," he said and handed me the keys. I gave him the biggest hug ever, I did not want to let him go. "Oh, but it is" I whispered in his ear, my lips softly touching his earlobe. Eddie released me from our embrace and placed his hand on my pregnant belly. "Now you look after yourself, and remember under no circumstances! no matter how hard it gets or how much you want to you must not contact me or the girls. Don't come near the flat or house ever."Eddies voice was firm but shaky he was looking me straight in the eyes, I could see he was upset. A tear rolled down my cheek. "Eddie I'm gonna miss you" my voice now a whisper as I try to hold back the tears. I plant a kiss on his cheek, and then on the lips, I wish I didn't have to let him go. Eddie kissed my pregnant belly.

I lifted my top showing my pregnant swell. "Touch it Eddie" my voice commanding

Eddie kissed my bare swollen belly making my loins tingle with pleasure. I wanted him one last time.

"Please Eddie I want you one last time" desperation quivering he scooped me up and walked into my bedroom.

" Eva I have to go, you will be fine ok you hear me you will be just fine you and the baby" and with that, he turned and walked down the stairs to the front door. He opened it without looking back and he was gone.

Reality hit me like a wave crashing on the sea wall. I was alone for the very first time in my life and it was a feeling I would grow to know. I lay back on my bed looking up at the bare ceiling, my feelings of loneliness overwhelming. I needed to keep myself busy and took to sorting out the flat, unpacking my belongings which did not consist of much other than my clothes and a few personal photos and gifts. I began to hang my clothes in the wardrobe, and folded my t-shirts, and placed them in the chest of drawers along with my underwear. I felt like I was playing house it was all so surreal I couldn't take it in. I told myself again."you are safe".Upon opening the second drawer I was shocked to see three piles of tiny clothing, baby grows and vests all in white, and little socks and booties. Eddie must have put them there along with everything else. I took one of the baby grows out and held it to my tummy my emotions overwhelming me, I sat on the end bed and cried. I really was going to have a baby soon, that I would cradle in my arms, whose forehead I would kiss so softly, whose tiny hand would curl around my finger. I lay the baby grow in the cot and tried to imagine my baby lying there. And then I felt the pain in my chest as I recalled holding her in my arms not wanting to let go, even though she was cold and not moving. I could hardly breathe as I choked back the tears and cradled my belly."I won't let you down I promise" I said to my growing baby.

I sat back on the bed letting the tears roll down my cheeks. I was so tired from it all. I really had escaped from him, I actually had done it, at last, I was free, no more pain or fear no more never again, but God did I miss him. I needed to sleep, to switch my mind off from all that was past."Your safe" I told myself, but I did not feel it. I clambered under the covers and tucked them tightly around me and drifted off to sleep.

I awoke startled many hours later it was dark I had slept so long and it took my eyes a while to become accustomed to my surroundings. I was alone! and I felt the unbearable pain of it. As I sat there in the dark I wanted him needed him to put his arms around me to kiss me to touch me in that way that only he could. The magnitude of it all came crashing around me, the choice that I had so bravely made weighing heavy on my heart and again I cried to myself.

I spent the next four months of my pregnancy crying myself to sleep and constantly looking over my shoulder, I was always afraid and he never left my mind. Being alone for the first time in my life and carrying his child was not easy. I wish I had someone to share it with, someone to talk to about it. But I knew I had to soldier on whatever because the life growing inside me was the fire that kept me living that kept me moving forward. It was the most precious thing in the world to me I had risked my life to carry this life inside me.

I wondered if he thought about me if he craved my touch if he had replaced me with another. My body still yearned for him, even to feel his hard fists beating me. I craved his touch no matter how brutal it was.

I couldn't remember a time when I hadn't been a sexual object when id been left alone with no one violating me, and it felt foreign but the fact that I could spend these months with my body to myself and enjoy my growing belly and the bond I was forming with this life growing inside was exactly what I needed to help me break away.

Lying in the bath relaxing, caressing my pregnant belly as my baby moved inside was the time of day I looked forward to the most. I felt so connected to this life growing inside of me and even though it pained me to think of his father my desire to care for this baby and give it the best I could outweigh the huge risk I had taken.

I pleasured myself most days and nights thinking of him always as I brought myself to climax, it was like releasing myself from some desperate torture, my sexual desires entangled with the choking feeling of loss. I would cry after and I still do sometimes, though I'm not sure why.

141

Birth

"They say you don't remember the pain of giving birth. They lie. I remember plenty. But they also say that it would all be worth it. And as I look in the eyes of my beautiful baby, I can tell you that they were right. On that count, at least."

During my last few months of pregnancy, I had reconciled my relationship with my mother, who was now playing the role of the eager grandparent. I was reluctant but glad to have her here in my life even though the relationship was dysfunctional. I needed someone for support and she seemed more than willing to give me that.

Mother had decided that as I only had three weeks till my due date it would be best if I moved in with her so she could be on hand at the given moment. I was happy to oblige and to soak up any care or comfort she offered me. She talked about the baby constantly to her friends and took a great amount of interest in every ache or pain or twinge I had and I reveled in it. For the first time, I felt a real bond between us and I was happy to have her in my life.

Three weeks seemed like a lifetime of waiting for this bundle so precious to me. But I was not going to have to wait any longer and exactly three weeks to my due date my baby boy was born.

I awoke in the early hours of the morning with a pain I had felt before and known all too well. I tossed and turned trying to sleep but the pain came again. Ten minutes apart then thirty minutes then five until I could not take anymore. This was definitely not a false alarm. I checked my watch it was now 5:30 am. Wrapping a dressing gown around me I got up and went upstairs to my mother's bedroom. I knocked on the door twice before opening it and stirring my mother. "Its started," I said "but the contractions are all over the place "

"come let's go and make some tea, it will probably be hours yet," she said matter of factly.

We headed downstairs where my mother filled and boiled the kettle whilst asking "is that another contraction?" to which I would reply "yes." We sat together in the dark waiting for it to get light sipping on our tea whilst my mother timed my contractions. They were painful but nothing compared to what I knew they would be. At 8:30 am mother decided that nothing much was going to happen for a while yet and that maybe I should try and sleep or at least rest and to let here know when the contractions became regular.

I took her advice and went back to bed saying I would meet her at the church she attended later that morning where they ran a coffee shop.

Bang!, bang! , bang! I awoke to my mother's front door being furiously knocked. Who the hell could that be I thought to myself and then realized I wasn't having any contractions and I had slept for three hours. I grabbed my dressing gown and wrapped it around me and went to see who was at the door. I was surprised to see my mother's friend standing there looking concerned and worried. "Are you ok?" she said letting herself through the front door.

"'I'm fine" I replied somewhat confused. "Your mothers worried sick. When you didn't show up at the church she thought that you may have been at home in labour by yourself and not know what to do so she sent me as I'm a midwife" her voice was rushed and panicky."I'm sorry I must have fallen asleep but the contractions seemed to have stopped now, I'll get dressed and go and meet her" I said chuckling to myself wondering what all the fuss was about.

We had coffee and then headed home about a fifteen-minute walk back to my mother's house, but as we started to walk down the hill the contractions started again, only this time thick and fast and I was struggling to walk. Mother was timing them." Yep definitely happening now," she said "they are eight minutes apart"

I managed a slow walk back to my mother's house and rang the maternity unit. I was trying to hide how scared I was of what was to come. Would I deliver a healthy baby or was I doomed to suffer yet another loss?

On arriving at the maternity unit I felt an overwhelming sense of fear and in trepidation. The place was so alien to me with all these midwives taking care of me and my mother at my side, so far removed from my previous experience crouched in my bathroom frightened and in pain and only to hold my dead baby in my arms so alone and lost I was. And now the pain of contractions seemed easier, maybe because of the knowledge I had of what was happening to my body. I felt at ease like I was meant to be there and I followed my instincts and listened

144

to what the midwives told me. I was still afraid but I was not alone.

The doctor examined me

"This isn't good," Doctor Johnor exclaimed. He widened his eyes. "It looks like something isn't right ."What does that mean?!" I yelled through my pain. I was told my baby was breech meaning he was upside down and that this would cause complications during birth but was reassured that all these people knew what they were doing. I was given gas and air to help with the contractions and my mother talked me through each one as they came closer together and stronger, I knew the time was coming and I was afraid but I knew I had to do this ."I got to throw up," I said. My body was hot, heavy, and in pain. I felt like the pain would never end. I held my mother's hand as another strong contraction came taking my breath away, the gas and air no longer helping. Everyone hovered around me like wild animals. I needed space. I needed air. "Get this thing out of me!" I shouted, squeezing my mother's hand tightly."It's fine, all you need to do is keep breathing." she soothed

If the baby didn't leave my body soon, I might faint. And at that moment it was like I just knew what to do. "I have to push" I cried out as the wave of contraction came again.

The room was filled with lots of medical staff a consultant and various other doctors and midwives but I was not afraid. The natural part of my womanhood guiding my instincts.

With the next contraction, the urge to push was overwhelming and I did not want to fight against it. I took a deep breath and with all my might pushed hard. The burning pain of my baby being born unbearable but I did not stop I held my mother's hand tightly and pushed again harder until my baby's bottom emerged. The pain was like pushing a watermelon through a hole the size of a lemon; it was like I was being ripped in half. The consultant made a small cut and gently guided his limbs out as I pushed again until all that remained was his head.

"Keep pushing, you're almost there," the doctor reminded me, and with another push, my baby was born and immediately wrapped in a blanket.

The midwife handed the bundle to me announcing "It's a boy" I placed him to my chest and wept. He was the most beautiful baby I had ever seen weighing 5lbs 4oz's he was crying and screwing his little face-up, and at that moment I felt the most amazing feeling of love for this tiny little human. My mother smiled a smile I will never forget one of such pride and such love for me, I smiled back at her "Look mum he's beautiful, he really is" and she nodded in agreement.

I took him to my breast he latched on with ease suckling away and I just couldn't stop looking at him. "Tobias, I'm going to call him Tobias," I said beaming with pride.

I just could not stop looking into his tiny scrunched up face he was so perfect so pure and innocent to all that had been part of his arrival into the world and I wondered if I was right to have brought him into this life of mine that was so battered and bruised, that carried scars that could never be healed. Or maybe this tiny being would heal them, maybe this was exactly what I needed, a love that was pure and unconditional to right all the wrongs.

The devil in me

It was not long before the ingrained desires in me came to the forefront. I found myself hooking up with anyone I could trying to satisfy the longing need I had only to find myself racked with pain and self-pity at my disgusting behavior. Each time I would tell myself that I would not degrade myself and let them violate me, but I was longing for the emptiness I felt to be filled and this was the only way I knew how.

I call it escorting now as it seems less dirty and degrading that way. I have four websites and a separate mobile for taking calls.

I get a call to go to a swanky address in Chelsea so cancel my lunch plans with friends. It's especially annoying when the job turns out to be for two twenty-year-old spoilt rich kids. When I arrive there's another escort there and everyone is taking drugs and doing shots.

The lads offer me extra cash for a foursome but I refuse so we split into pairs. My bloke makes me perform on him for ages. He's not dangerous just arrogant and obnoxious.

When I dislike a client I just detach and go through the motions. My mind starts wandering about what's on tv tonight.

I was irritated by those who so-called loved me as if anyone could love me. I did not want their desire or devotion to me ."What fools !"I would say to myself laughing at their determined need of me if they only knew how I detest them, how I loathe their touch on my skin.

They think they know me, that we share some kind of sexual chemistry, but I spit at your craving for me. I laugh to myself at your lack of sexual ability. How all of you wish to make me climax, how needy you become when I come close, and how obsessed you are in your endeavors. I toy with you like a cat with a mouse taunting you until you give up and die, not literally no that would be far too easy.No you leave me, but still wanting more and I dangle temptation like a carrot on a string just enough to keep you.

My favorite game is the one where you tell me all about what she won't do for you and how you long to try these things out, how bored you are of your relationship, and its boundaries. Then here am I willing to let you and just like that you are hooked and I'm reeling you into my net.

In these times my face is smiling as you penetrate me anally and I know I have won the game. You enter me cautiously at first concerned that you will hurt me and still in disbelief that your fantasy is about to be fulfilled. But soon your cock pushes further and harder inside me awakening something deep and evil, and the moans that come from my mouth seem so real to you. I'm looking at my watch hoping the excitement of it all will bring you quickly to ejaculation so I can get this over with.

I feel nothing you see but pain and anguish at myself, at this person that lives deep within me that has no concept of real love or the world she lives in. We torment each other with our actions.

I ride your desperate cocks moaning loudly pushing myself down hard onto them arching my back, your hands on my breasts. My fingers enter your mouths and you suck on them as I bring your cocks to climax.

You tie me up and watch me squirm as you tease me or give me pain. You hit me hard with your belt buckle and I cry out a lust-filled gasp. You climb on top of me entering me your hands squeezing around my throat my cries and whimpers, my shouting to stop bringing you closer to the edge. Your grip tightens you squeeze my throat harder as your last force full thrusts rip into my vagina and your release fills me. I cry out too the pretense so easy for me to do it fools you.

I am possessed by something, she lies deep inside me waiting and waiting for me to let her out. She does not like it down in the deep dark depths of my soul. She longs to see the light. She wants more time to play with your souls, feeding on them until she can be free again. She is the devil inside me.

At this point, she has no name.

Chameleon

Throughout my adolescence, I felt shackled by the chains of society and weighed down by the opinions of my peers and the reputation they had cast on me since the day I was caught performing oral on a boy at school. I wouldn't be one of the people who was forgot, I would not be labeled as unoriginal or unimportant.

I wanted to be new go where someone didn't know me, I could become anyone, but who was I going to be? how would I define this new person?

I had tried being the free-spirited slut that wore crop tops and shorts, but I had no idea who I was and friends referred to me as a hot mess.

I began to copy other people's personality traits. Things I liked, tones of voice, hairstyle, dress sense, behavior. Every change I made took me further away from that little girl I once was, yet nothing made me feel better at about myself.

To me sex was never and had never been about my desires or needs it was always about being who the other person wanted me to be. I was like a relational/sexual chameleon, I was a trained performer in this area. It was the only thing I felt I was good at.

After working as a prostitute my respect for men was destroyed, I became hard-hearted towards them, I didn't know how to relate to them in anything other than a sexual way, I didn't trust them, didn't like them in fact I would say that I eventually began to hate them, but strangely I still wanted to find someone I could love and who could love me.

Was I just going through some phase that I should have gone through in my teenage years?

As with anyone I'm sure I was just trying to find my identity, but I'm not sure that this is just a phase. Everybody has thoughts of starting over but I wanted to wake up a different person. I wanted to be so open-minded exposed to so many stimuli that this would influence my thoughts and I could forget the dark places I had been. I thought that these thoughts if sustained would turn into actions which in turn would become habits and those habits would become beliefs.

Would I ever run out of creative ideas? Writer's block "Nah!"

My open-mindedness gave me new ideas, new ways of talking, but I had to keep shifting my beliefs.I could easily change myself on the outside, but on the inside, I was becoming lost.

I would feel new even reborn like I had lived several lifetimes, but the feeling was fleeting and so my chameleon would have to change colour again. It was incredibly satisfying at first showing up in front of people that knew me as a different person with a new way of processing life's challenges, it was empowering.

constantly reinventing myself, meant I was never really that person. I would end up creating thousands of blog posts, articles, videos, and more, but at no point was the "old reliable" or "tried and true", me ever-present. When you constantly show up as a different version of yourself people don't know what to expect and feel they cant count on you.

I felt like after doing this so many times I was snapping back to my former self like an elastic band and my constant visions of grandeur leading me to believe I was the coolest woman alive were wearing thin because I wasn't more,I wasn't better and I certainly was not different for it. I am who I am. All I can do is get to know myself better. It's like peeling away the layers and masks that act as a disguise and protective mechanism.

I was living in a constant state of discomfort for trying to change me inside and out. Transformation felt good but everything leading up to it felt bad. Was it just a habit? or was it part of my identity, is it because of deep-seated insecurities experienced in my past? Am I just addicted to that feeling?

There is no shame in casting off your past and your old self. There is no shame in leaving your old self behind and creating someone completely new. Just make sure you are doing it for the right reasons and that the person you are becoming is continually gaining respect.

I just didn't know how or where to start with becoming who I really was.

In my opinion, my brain is my worst enemy. I sound crazy but it's true. It tells me degrading things I don't want to hear. It makes me think about things I don't want to think about. It shows me images that I don't want to see. It plays me horrible scenarios of the future, like my family and friends dying or being severely depressed or them just forgetting about me, leaving me alone, and battling with my mental health.

152

When I look in the mirror I despise what I see and have cut myself because of it and have even considered going anorexic, even though I know the consequences and the pain I would be in. When I eat my brain says insults to me.

my fucked up mind.

My name is Eva & I am probably the most complicated person. I don't know what that means, but it means something.

It's like I work against myself, if I know something is gonna bother me my mind wants to do it, why the fuck, also I get weird feelings, anybody else? and like I'm so conscious of sounds and what people around me do, it's so stressful, I just want to end this all

Looking in the mirror and I can see all my demons.

Telling me to just stop all my fucking dreaming.

Voices in my head telling me to give up.

Smoking more weed and pouring liquor inside my cup.

Drowning out the noise, it seems to be getting louder.

More criticism instead of them getting prouder.

So I'm sitting here analyzing all their shit.

Every day a new struggle how do I put up with it.

I need something to do, got a hard decision to choose.

Because I'm fighting not to let all my demons loose.

So I made my decision, yeah I'm fucking done.

Go back to the spot needed to buy some guns.

Put everyone else out of my misery.

Even if they are old or young.

Tell me where I went wrong.

Voices told me to set it off so I fucking set it off.

Killing all the innocent, make it another mass murder incident.

Sound of the gun sounding like an instrument.

Tell me where I go now?

Police surrounding me telling me put my guns down and come out with my hands up.

So I go find a private room and I sit in the ground.

Gun to my head I think I'm on my last round.

Now the demons are quiet, they got what they wanted.

New voices in my head, voices of the dead I think I'm being haunted.

Mind running everywhere this life is getting exhausting.

Don't know what to do, I got nothing to lose.

Refuse to go to jail, refuse to live that life,

refuse to face my consequences, refuse to accept what is wrong, and what is really right.

Police getting closer I hear them coming south,

time to pull the trigger blow all my brains fucking out.

Run from the voices that are in my fucking head.

Mind of a mass murderer, study it when I'm dead.

God wants me dead too your not special

Why am I here? I ask myself, what is my purpose?

I think I'm so special but I'm not God wants me dead too, because he knows the evil that lies within me and he cannot let it live.

I admit, there are times when I believe God enjoys bringing pain into my life. I know in my head that God works all things for good, and that I am supposed to rejoice always, and that nothing can blady, blady, blah. But deep down, I suspect God somehow enjoys seeing me suffer. I think of God as a drill sergeant. He makes me suffer because He knows it will ultimately be truly good for me. But he also makes me suffer because he enjoys seeing me break down. I imagine that God enjoys breaking me.

I gulp down the pills each handful becoming harder for me to swallow, but I must continue. I've lost count now as I become drowsy, my hand shaking on the bottle of vodka I hold. My thoughts are racing, my heart is racing, I feel the sweat on my face, but I must continue. I lose myself for a time locked in this cycle of swallowing, my throat is trying to stop me from gulping down the bitterness of the tablets the burning of the vodka, but I must continue.

God definitely wants me dead I'm sure of it, am I?

How can I be so cruel, so selfish to wish to leave this life to leave him lying in his cot crying out for me only for his cries to be unanswered? He sobs until his tiny body is exhausted. I can't leave him to die alone without me I must call for help. My mind is now swimming in guilt and confusion I hear his cries and know I must go to him, I must pick him up and cradle him in my arms soothing him. He cannot look after himself he's a child an innocent who must not be scared by my inability to survive this life. I must get up God does not want me dead, I have not come this far just to slip away before life even has the chance to blossom.

I clamber to the phone my body heavy and immobile and dial the number 999. The caller hears his cries and my lucid tones and then I see the flashing of blue and red.

I will live to see another day.

And now I have more shame and guilt to carry the burden weighs heavy but I carry it like the chains that already shackle me its harder to get up to move forward, but that fire inside me fuels me and so I smile and take joy in the beauty of the life I have created and he alone gives me the strength to stand up.

My Dad Told My Mom To Create Chaos So She Made Me

Maybe the unknown was scarier than the known, but I mostly think my silence was due to shame. I lived in shame and took the responsibility on my own shoulders.

My dad's a bit of a drinker. It's how I get my bruises. And, theoretically, my self-induced scars. But, what hurts worse is the insecurity. The internal brokenness that only a person exposed to abuse can experience. It's like this: those mental scars are a tapering factor in the serenity of domestic life. They cause agony that can only be seen on the inside. The pain that no one else sees because… well, no one else cares

There were nights I lay in my bed listening to the sound of fighting. My mother would shout, my father would begin laying into her and the screaming would start. She cried, he seethed, and I pushed my face into the long toy snake my three-year-old body was wrapped around. I would think to myself how when mother left I would leave with her, flee the violence.

Then one day he left... and I remained right where I was with just a toy to comfort me.

However, growing up in the pre-Internet age, it felt as if I was the only one living with an abusive, alcoholic father. The only one whose mother chose to remain curled into herself instead of protecting her child. The only one who flicked a bathroom light on and waited before entering the room.

The Incubus was lurking in all the dark corners or hiding under my bed.

Dad,

I don't even want to call you that. You are not a dad, you are not a parent. You have never been a dad to me. I think when I was really young I wanted your attention and I wanted you to be proud of me, but by the time I started going to school, I began wishing I had a different dad. I think I actually believed that it would be better to have no dad because I was convinced they were all like you. I see you as a monster. I haven't seen you for almost 2 years, and I haven't lived under your roof for many more and yet you still appear in my nightmares.

A door slammed causes me to jump and be transported back in time. I won't speak with you on the phone because your voice, your words, shake me to my core. I hate you. I hate you for making me hate you, for filling me with such sadness and rage. I hate you for causing me to hate myself, for making me believe I am nothing. You are a vile and cruel person. I am ashamed of you. The weight is immense. I am terrified that somewhere in me a part of you exists. I don't want to be anything like you. You make me sick. In the past, being in your presence or even hearing from you made me want to purge. I used to starve myself for days on end, scratch my throat and purge blood in some twisted effort to eliminate you from my life, to express how tortured I felt inside. Anger welling up in me and no safe place to go. A peaceful sleep eludes me. Sometimes I feel as though I am living through everything all over again. I wake up in the middle of the night, crying and disoriented I feel my heart pounding as I ran down the street barefoot and in pyjamas , praying to God that I would make it to my friends place safely. I see broken glass, holes in walls, doors pulled off hinges... destruction everywhere.

From the outside, our place always looked so pleasant but I think people knew that things were not perfect. So many secrets... even now. I am so sensitive to sound and movement now, craving a silent and nurturing calm that feels constantly out of reach. Your voice. Your thunder. Your red-in-the-face, slurring, filthy mouth. Everything you did was so loud and frightening to me. To this day the sound of a key in a lock puts me on edge.I see you naked on the floor in the bathroom in a pool of your own vomit. I am disgusted that you think it's funny to flash yourself in your bathrobe or worse. I hear bottles of booze, I see them stashed around the house. I am ashamed that you hurt me, I try to fight the thoughts that tell me it must be my fault but they overpower me. I wonder if maybe i am cursed.

I learned to dissociate at an early age. I could leave my body any time I wanted. In fact, I disowned my body entirely. I wasn't that person with the mean father. I didn't want to be her. I couldn't be her. Knowing you and all that you have done makes me want to sink into the floor and disappear from sight.

I used to numb out the pain you caused. At least I was in control. I wanted to rid myself of the sickness I felt inside me after being around you. I bet you don't even remember this. I don't believe you have any interest in ever taking inventory

159

of all the harm you have done, all the times you hurt me. I considered killing myself because of how ashamed you made me feel and how helpless I felt. You made life a living hell. There was never any peace, not one single day.

You won't even recognize the hell you created to this day.

I can have empathy for my father, I can even acknowledge that he was not bad all the time and that's what makes it all so complicated, why its all so confusing, why over time I learned to brace myself for what might come next because his good mood one second could switch to an abusive one the next.

He made me feel like I was worthless that my life didn't matter. I'm slowly learning that I do matter I am not garbage and as I believed most of my life.

Incubus

Writing is the monster that lives beneath my floorboards. The one I incessantly feed for fear it may turn and devour my soul. Writing is the friend who doesn't return my phone calls; the itch I'm unable to scratch; a dinner invitation from a cannibal. Writing

isn't something that makes me happy like a good cup of coffee. It's just something I do because not writing, as I've found, is so much worse.

Eenie ,meenie,miney,mo which one shall I be today?

Ever since I was very young, I would hear, in my head, other people talking, but I knew it was me, in a way. I knew that some part of me that wasn't quite me was telling me things, but growing up, I thought that was normal, because I watched Pinocchio, and they tell you about the conscience, and how the conscience is the little voice in your head telling you right from wrong. I named these voices, and over time they began to develop beyond an imaginary friend or the voice of your conscience that's telling you, "Don't play with your mom's makeup."

When I look back, I had one personality who would always go to the therapy sessions. She would always tell the therapist things were going well, because [for her], everything was good. She wasn't conscious of the issues I was having. But I knew I was still having issues and problems, and I felt like I was deliberately lying to the therapist. The rest of my personalities would be like, Why would I say that? Why would I lie when I know things aren't good?

I had become incredibly detached from reality, because all my different parts, were so disconnected from each other, I couldn't tell what was a dream, if I was really awake, or if the experience of one personality was a true experience because you feel like it didn't happen to you. If one of my personalities was out getting drunk and being promiscuous, I might have a vague memory of having sex, but it's like watching a movie — a movie you're not very invested in because you forget the details and it's boring.

I think I've started to become unhinged *Am I awake right now? Is any of this real? Am I here? Is anyone here?* At a certain point, I felt like, *Maybe I'm a god, or I'm some sort of deity, or I'm a ghost* because I felt so far removed from a sense of physicality because of dissociation.

It's like a numbing of the senses so you don't have to feel the intensity of an experience. Everyone experiences dissociation to a degree. If you've ever gotten in a car and driven somewhere but you don't remember how you got there. It's an autopilot mode, where you shut down the focus and the details of life so you can just get something done. It was like that, but all the time. I'd walk around, go to the bathroom, eat my food, get dressed — but I felt like I wasn't there. I wasn't present, I couldn't feel things. I would injure myself and not even know I was injured until I saw blood because I couldn't feel pain. I had very little sense of time. It all felt like the same time. I started getting scared.

I'm Sarah. I am, I guess, the more responsible one. I'm the one who spoke to our therapists in the past and told them everything was going swimmingly, not knowing there were others in my head having a difficult time.

Eva(she is my teenage self) is not good at speaking technically about things. She most likely would find the conversation overwhelming, so then Sarah comes in to protect her senses, and then to basically continue the conversation, like I understood the content of this conversation in more depth than Eva does.

Every personality has its own strengths and weaknesses. For example, Eva is much friendlier and great at socializing, and very likable, but she is a child so she loses focus easily…Sarah is great with managing responsibilities — she's the married one with children and grandchildren the one who has had a career and been successful. She has the highest anxiety of our personalities.

You know how sometimes you just feel a little angry inside, but you can ignore it, but it's something in the back of your head? It would be like deciding, I have this anger, and I'm going to focus it and allow it to be expressed. She's like a tornado of pain and trauma she cannot control She's the one who always gets hurt.

Sarah is very responsible. She sounds the most adult. She sounds our age. She has a really high work ethic and good morals, and she always wants to do things the right way. She's a bit of a perfectionist — *a lot* of a perfectionist — and she has OCD. Because of that, she gets really easily overwhelmed. She'll set really high expectations, and if she doesn't meet them, she gets upset with herself.

Amid the confusing, terrifying mingling of different voices in one consciousness comes memories of child abuse, the first episode occurring when she was three, "I have no proof," I note. "I have to go with what I believe happened, and my reality."

I have lots of adult parts. Development should be seamless… But because I didn't grow up naturally, I would update myself… Finally, there were five different adult parts, each managing a stage of my adult life.

If you're in a totally impossible situation, you dissociate to stay alive. Trauma can freeze you in time.

I suppose I split myself into parts so I could cope, one part to endure the abuse and contain the horrific emotional and physical impact. The other that gets up in the morning and carries on, and many other different parts that splinter off. My consciousness is trying to keep Eva safe.

And so I behave differently depending on who is in my mind.

I remain, Eva, until another takes over. My memories are blunted normal emotion subdued leaving me unable to cope with the trauma. The lack of emotion has never left me like I know I'm doing things but it's like I'm watching it happen to me.

Now the incubus he's the one that enters my dreams at night terrifying me leaving me screaming and physically fighting for my life.

I can't fall asleep on my back, or rather I do not dare to, I often slip into a state where my mind wakes up from a dream, but my body remains immobile. In this state I can still sense things around me, sunlight trickling through the curtains, passerby on the street below, the covers hanging onto the floor. But when I tell myself to get up I cannot move. I fight and struggle to stretch my arms or wiggle a toe but it's no good. Then I begin to panic. Being awake, my mind expects my lungs to take full, hearty breaths, to feel my throat expanding, and my sternum rising a good six inches. But my body — still asleep, physiologically — takes mere sips of air. I feel I'm suffocating, bit by bit, and panic begins to smolder in my chest.

The other is you wake in a sweat, heart beating rapidly, and stare in terror as something sinister approaches your bed. You scream for it to go away. You thrash out wildly, but it still advances, evil oozing from its shapeless form. It approaches my bed and climbs in next to me touching me, hurting, me, lying heavily on top of me, I shout out again and then I wake.

Sunshine and Rainbows Usually Mean Happiness, Right?

❦

I've met someone and I think I might be in love. Some well-wishers have told him I am a prostitute, but he does not care. we are in love and I think it's mutual. He has taken me away from everything and we are practically living together. He stays at mine during the week and at the weekend I stay at his. I've introduced him to Joshua and he adores him. He says there is no need to talk about my past and we dream of getting old together, falling asleep on the same pillow. I am happy every second of every day and I really feel that this could be it for me.

Wrapped up in all this bliss I do not seem to notice the little red flags. My desperate need to be loved, happy and live a normal life is a rose-coloured tint I see the world around me in.

Can I really be this naive? surely not? But sadly I am, I still cling on to a hope that I will be saved and that all that went before was just some god-awful nightmare that I will wake from.

I carried on blissfully unaware of the pitfuls clinging onto the dream of a real family and so I married Duncan and he became the best father to my son that I could have wished for.

From the outside, it was a perfect marriage, yet I hid the purple "flowers" that blossomed over my legs. On skin as pale as mine, it was harder to hide, but it was there and I felt the pain with each breath. Our home was a cage for my body and in my depression, my body began to feel like a cage for my soul.

His hand hit and I felt the force of it. The first slap, seven years ago, had been the worst. I hadn't expected him to be so strong but there was weight and strength enough to stun. Though his hand was empty, it was like being hit with a hunk of meat nonetheless, and afterward, I would endure his words of hatred, all spilling from a man that professed so much love in his quiet moments of regret. every facet of my personality was denigrated and shunned.I was less than nothing, not even loved as much as a used object. Every look filled with contempt and annoyance. Once I had been beautiful and thin and the envy of other men. Now I had gained a few pounds after the birth of our third child.I was nothing but another ugly woman lying in these sheets. The laughter of our youth was dead, the house cramped and noisy. Love had turned to hate, a hatred so potent.

When he was angry he would lash out at me, watching me crumble with grim satisfaction.

You didn't choose me to love or cherish, but to whip and destroy - for power and malice are your drugs of choice. They light you up inside with a sickly glow that shines in those languid eyes.

I fell back into my old ways looking to seek comfort from others. The prostitute in me was back.

I was one of those who told all the clients how lovely it is to see them, how happy I am to work with them, how they are my favorite clients. I really tried to make myself believe it too.

The truth is, of course, I was very happy to see their money, and I was also very happy to see them leave me alone after our sessions. Cheerfully shouting at them as they left: "Thanks! I had a great time! Welcome back!"

Which in fact meant: "Thanks for the money so I can survive another day, I'm so happy that it's over for today. But I will never get out of this misery, so I must try to keep my regulars happy to avoid the risks that come with meeting new clients."

And I was often told by clients that my "Girlfriend Experience" was awesome, almost perfect. "Just an illusion or was it real?" This was asked sometimes. I was often told that I was wholeheartedly involved with my clients in our sessions. That my pleasure was not fake, that I really seemed to love sex.

169

I promoted myself as a girl next door. I'd wear very light make-up and flat shoes or Converse. I'd sometimes get requests for "something slutty", but I didn't have a problem with that – it can be fun to get out of my skin. When I'd meet someone for the first time, I wouldn't know what they like so I'd just morph at the moment. It's quite intuitive: I try to work out whether they want someone strong with political views, or someone more girlish. It can be a lot of fun to work with people's desires, things that they think are too perverse to tell a partner. When clients ask to go bareback, i would be scared: there are certain positions where they could just take the condom off. If I felt like they were a risk, I wouldn't see them again – unless I needed the money, which happened a lot.

What sex? I have no memories of the sex part at all, they are all suppressed under the well-practiced performance. The performance that helped me survive in this world since I was thirteen.

The clients wondered if there were actually some real, hot feelings between us. Many messages from them, thanking me for the experience. And I never even remembered what had happened. I felt like a robot every day. But seems that I really was a good actress.

The clients of course wouldn't know better, because I was always on drugs and alcohol, and I had blocked my mind from remembering too much, to protect my inner self, like most of us do in prostitution.

I would sit there afterward looking at the money thinking how much more I needed so I could be free of this life and run off into the sunset. I thought if I could get rich the happiness of money would erase all the memories of my past.

I had no education no job.No work experience other than that in the sex industry. My life felt like one big lie. I had four beautiful children who knew nothing of the horror that lay behind their mother's face. Life was a constant battle of juggling the different parts of me, mother, wife, friend, prostitute!

I was so desperate to protect my family, but I felt like I ruined everything I touched. All I could focus on was just getting the motivation to go on living, to breathe, to keep my mask from slipping. I was demanding, cheating, clingy and disrespectful.

I was going to stop as soon as I had enough money, no more lies, I could start over again with my husband and the kids. But it's hard when your always lonely, ashamed, and feel it's all your fault. All the trauma and negative feelings all the flashbacks are all my fault.I kept telling myself it was okay and that there was nothing really wrong with me.

But I knew there was, what was it I was searching for because I would not find happiness here.No rich client was going to sweep me off his feet.

And prostitution is not a job. The insides of a woman are not a workplace.

When I started seeing my husband, I was a 19-year-old depressed girl with family problems. I had weak health, poor self-confidence – it was as if I was wearing an "abuse me" sticker.

Right from the beginning, I knew that something was wrong, but my intuition was silenced by the hunger for love I had. Later in our relationship, I realised clearly that I was suffering but I wasn't able to identify the source. It was standing next to me and I was calling it love.

Being in the relationship was like being locked in a prison, being tied up, and unable to speak. Sometimes when we were out together I "disappeared" for the whole evening and curled in a nook. I felt better away from him, away from his mordant words. My eating habits were never okay, but with him, at times I wasn't able to eat at all, as he used to scold me in restaurants and even at home for "bad table manners". I was a sociable person but by the time I met him, I was an alone freak Gradually he made me believe that I have no friends. If I had any, I wouldn't introduce him to them because I was so afraid of being embarrassed. So he discouraged me from making friends and on the other hand, he criticised me for being a loner. Later I read in a psychology book that this is called a "double bind", a manipulation.

There were many obvious signs that he didn't care about me: he didn't keep promises, he didn't look out for me. I apologised for him, believing the excuses he gave me. I did everything for him and he hardly ever thanked me. I was intelligent compared to him but he never wanted to hear anything about my successes. He accused me of hurting him and showing off. He was The King in my eyes and the loser was always me.

Then there was also a great confusion in my head about our sexual relationship. I thought that everything was okay even though I remember myself going home in pain. He didn't care about my feelings. I thought my sex life was just okay but later I developed post-traumatic syndrome and gynecological problems.

I remember he could get furious about just anything and start to yell and kick things. Once he called me bad names just because he couldn't find his keys. Another time I was helping him with his work and he wouldn't stop shouting at me. Was I the one to blame for his aggressiveness? Sure I was. I believed that if I had behaved well, he wouldn't have got angry.

We never argued in the true sense of the word. He had his requirements and I submitted.

It was the third Christmas when our relationship started to break. I was so afraid of losing him that I would negotiate his insane accusations and try to submit. He didn't like that I was a "sociable person" (i.e. drinking with friends), that I wore wear make-up like the other girls, and that we didn't have much in common (which was true, no matter how hard I tried to resemble him).

The trap was that he was so different from the first relationship that I thought he must be a decent guy. He wasn't. I start to tremble when I saw him even now. I called him a vampire and that's precisely what he was.

He made me stay up late and tortured me with endless negotiations about "his uncertainty whether he wants to be with me or not". He never had time for me and would rather go with his friends to the pub to "help them to solve their emotional problems." This personality trait he seemed so proud of turned out to be an utter falsehood. He would smile at everybody else except me. I saw in his eyes several times that he didn't really see me as a human being. I have in my life felt so deeply terrified although there was nothing obviously violent in his behavior...

When I look back it's easy to see that my relationship was abusive from the start and followed a text-book pattern. Initially, my husband was fun, complimentary, encouraging, understanding - all the things you would want in a partner. I told him things I wouldn't tell anyone else; I felt like he was really trustworthy and had my back. *He liked the idea that I had a shady past of prostitution and when we got together I stopped at*

173

his request.

That really good phase lasted about nine months, but I realise now that it was a made-up fantasy, and the person he presented to hook me in doesn't exist. The compliments turned into insults; "you're so good at your job" turned into "you're so condescending, you're such a know it all". Really personal information I had told him became things to twist and throwback at me as evidence I was f*cked up and dysfunctional.

I was so stuck, I kept thinking that if I changed how I was, 'supported' him better (code for doing everything he wanted and not questioning it) kept going through this tricky phase, etc that things would go back to the way they were at the beginning. I know everyone says that - I think it's because they're so good at convincing you their behaviour is all your fault.

Over time the relationship became so abusive and destructive I was drinking and using drugs to try and deal with how I felt. I withdrew from friends and family, gave up my job, and was emotionally unavailable to my children as I was so pre-occupied with trying to please him I'd lost all sense of myself. I felt like a shell with nothing inside, like I would be sitting on the sofa with people around me talking and there was nothing left of me there, who I was didn't exist anymore.

I would do my own thing at home trying to ignore him. If he started nagging at me or whatever I would get in the car and go for a drive or go visit Mum's place or friends – just to get away from him. When I got back home he would be sweet for a while then he would be back to the old nasty person.

The abuse was mainly verbal and psychological but there were peaks of physical and sexual violence that kept me in fear of him all the time and I thought a few times that he was going to kill me.

If we had a few good days, I'd be waiting for it to change as I knew it wouldn't last. The constant fear made me anxious all the time, having panic attacks and crying at everything. I was too scared to tell anyone how bad it was so I just kept everything bottled up.

The bleeding had been going on for some weeks, and with it came the arguments. I was disgusting to him. Why? I ask because we couldn't have sex. At this stage in our marriage, we were still having sex two or three times a week. Maybe more if I counted the times he fucked me in my sleep.

I really can't recall how it all began. The bleeding had stopped and I was feeling better. He hadn't seemed to notice though. I kept my self busy going out with my friends to my local most nights. As soon as he returned from work I'd be off out the door, and id stay out until the pubs closed. I was lonely very lonely.

I arrived home late and went straight to bed. This was the norm as I had usually had quite a bit to drink. He was already asleep and so I did not bother myself with trying to wake him for sex as I knew he would ignore me and I would feel that dreadful feeling of rejection.

I must have been asleep for some time before I realised he had woken and gone downstairs. What was he doing down there? I asked myself. I lay there in the dark tossing and turning unable to rest, and so I got up and walked quietly downstairs.

I was not shocked at what I saw I was angry. There was my husband watching porn and masturbating. The fury inside me spilled out of nowhere. "I'm right here !" I shouted . "what the fuck is wrong with you it's been six weeks and I'm right here!"

175

tears streaming down my face I ran back upstairs slamming the bedroom door.

I heard his footsteps coming up the stairs and was already waiting for the onslaught of hateful words that were going to be said. I was not ready for what actually happened next.

He flew in through the bedroom door calling me a disgusting, ugly whore. " I don't want to have sex with a filthy bleeding woman, you've been like it for weeks!" he was shouting right into my face is moth a centimeter away from my nose. His eyes glazed over and wild.

Before I knew it he had grabbed me and slammed me hard into the bedroom door. I screamed out at him opening the door and running downstairs.

I would call my mother I thought or the police. I grabbed my mobile phone from my handbag, my hands shaking trying to unlock it to dial my mothers' number. The phone was flung from my hand landing on the floor. I pushed him away and grabbed it clutching it tightly in my hand so he couldn't get it from me. The punches to my head came thick and fast along with his hate full words. Then his hands were around my neck squeezing it so I couldn't breathe. This was it I was going to die, he was intent on killing me. I cried out for my mother pleading that I couldn't breathe and I didn't want to die. He released his grip and continued his insults and punching me in the head. And then something changed he did not look the same and I was afraid as he put his forearm on my neck and pushed down with all his bodyweight.

I was losing consciousness when the banging on the front door, and the sound of the police "we are coming in!" came. Startled he jumped up heading towards the door to find my son aged 15 fumbling to unlock the door to let them in crying and talking on his mobile phone. Realisation hit and my husband grabbed my son to stop him. I had to do something, so I stepped in between them trying to protect my son. Again I heard the police officers saying they were coming in and in a second the door was broken down and officers had my husband pinned down on the hallway floor.

I sat halfway up the stairs crying in shock and holding my son "thank you" was all I could say. He had saved my life.

I later discovered I had made headlines in the local newspaper, picking my kids up from school that day took more courage than I had left. I was their mother I had to find the courage and so, as usual, I waited in the school playground for the end of day bell to ring. My legs shaking my heart thumping in my chest I tried to not let it show, but the whispering voices amongst the playground parents proved what I had feared. The judgment in their facial expressions I wanted the ground to swallow me up.

Driving away from the school carpark rage building up inside me I wished I could just drive off into oblivion. Everyone knew how much I had and still was cheating on my husband, many of the school mums husbands had acquired my services so I knew that I deserved their looks of disdain. I felt a black cloud of shame over me as my parenting was put to the jury.

A scream came from nowhere, my children sat in the backseats looking upset and unsure. I pulled over on the side of the street, undoing my seatbelt and launching myself into the backseats to embrace my children. I needed to do better for them I told myself as we cried together. And so the mask returned to my face.

It's quite a terrible thing to admit that you have been in two abusive relationships. Confessing that though, I must add that

177

calling the things right names is the first big step in recovery. Ironically, when I met my second boyfriend, I was quite aware that my previous relationship had been abusive but I wasn't able to realiSe that things were going the same way again. I wanted love so much that I denied all signs right from the beginning.

The police I've met through all of this were really nice and supportive, but they don't realise how hard it is when someone you've loved or who you have children with is abusive. It really messes with your head and is not as simple as dealing with any other crime.

Even after that incident, he managed to get me back in his life, once the attention of the police went away he got in touch and told me how sorry he was and how much he loved me and put huge amounts of pressure on me. Really I think it was that he wanted me to drop the charges and make sure he didn't get convicted and knew he had to get me back on side.

Sometimes I would sit in my car crying hysterically thinking "please someone save me".

I had to change ,become part of society ,I needed to get a job and be a good mother.

Guess who is the happiest person on the whole earth, in the whole galaxy, in all of God's creation? It's me! I applied for the job of administrator and they offered me the position of an interview with Julie, my boss-to-be, and the girl from their HR department whose name I don't remember went smooth. They liked my confidence they were so friendly and smiled so heartily.

They said I can come to the office tomorrow. I swear that the grass had never smelled grassier and the sky had never seemed so high.

My first day at the office was kind of exhausting really. I'm so conscious of my mask slipping Am I really going to be able to do this without the cracks appearing that i know are there.

Oh please, Diary, help me to be strong and consistent. Help me to exercise every morning and night to be thin, take care of my skin till it gets absolutely flawless and petal smooth and clear, dress like a fashion model, eat right, and be optimistic and agreeable and positive and cheerful. I want to be important so much! Maybe the new me will be different.

Nobody will know my little secret. Don't you think that when something is going well, everything else goes well too?

Oh, dear Diary, I'm sorry I've neglected you, but I've been so busy. I have had a cold for the last week. I tried really hard to hide it and continued to go to the office. High temperature and terrible headache slowed me down, so I had to stay late to get the work done on time.

When I bought you, Diary, I was going to write diligently in you every day, but I'm writing all the time now except for the time I fall asleep. It becomes more and more difficult for me to fall asleep. I am constantly thinking about work and what I need to do tomorrow. Some days nothing happens and other days I'm too busy or too bored or too angry or too annoyed, or just to me to do anything I don't have to do.

I think I'm a pretty lousy friend even to you. Anyway, I feel closer to you than I do to even Megan who is my very best friend. Even with her, I'm not really me. I'm partly somebody else trying to fit in and say the right things and do the right things and be in the right place and wear what's trending. Sometimes I think I am just a shadow of real me, trying to do the same things even if I don't like them.

People are like robots off an assembly line, and I don't want to be a robot!

Oh Diary, it was miserable! The office has become the loneliest, coldest place in the world. Not one single person spoke to me during the whole endlessly long day. I came to Tracy and said I had a problem with my back. Then I left early and went by the pub and had a pint of lager, and then another and another. There had to be something in life that was worthwhile. I hated myself for being drunk all the time.

I guess I deserve it, but I am suffering! I ache even in my fingernails and toenails and in my hair follicles.

Oh, happiness and joy and elation! I've finally found a friend at the office. She's as loopy and misfitting as I am. We are chatting all the time and can't get enough of each other. It's unbelievable but I became more productive notwithstanding all these endless talks with her. Maybe I'm falling in love…

I was drunk me again last night. I don't even remember what time I came home.

My son is 16 today. I had no time to bake a cake for him, so I brought one from the shops. I am an awful mom

The office was a nightmare. After our yesterday's talk, when Sam understood that I'm totally in love with her, I was afraid I'd made everything so awkward. I hoped she was not at work. I pretended I didn't care, but oh, Diary, you even can't imagine how much I do! I care so much that it burns when I breathe; it feels like the dawn of the dead, like bombs going off in my head.

My whole insides have shattered

I feel so miserable and embarrassed and humiliated and beaten that's it's a great surprise I still function, still talk and smile and concentrate. Why do I do this to me? No, I am not going to talk about it I will pretend nothing happened. I'll never measure up to her expectations anyway.

180

Not sure what date it is. The last thing I remember is that I fell down right on the office floor. I am at the hospital now; the diagnosis is completely mental and physical debilitation. They stuff me with drugs. I am sleeping almost all the time.

Will write here later. Feel too tired and empty inside to continue.

Finally, I got out of the hospital. They prescribed me a heap of pills and told me not to smoke, drink alcohol, I should also visit my doctor ... But who the hell are they to tell me what to do???

P.S. I need to buy another diary as you are already filled.

I nearly died three weeks after my decision not to keep another diary. Duncan came home from friends and found me half-alive. He called an ambulance, and the doctors managed to bring me back to life again.

The doctor prescribed me sleeping pills again. I'm never going to be able to sleep without them. I don't need the sleep as much as I need the escape. It's a wonderful way to getaway. I just take a pill and wait for sweet nothingness to take over. At this stage in my life nothingness is a lot better than somethingness.

It's too bad that the sleeping pills lose their strength when you take them for a long period. I have to take two of these and sometimes even three. Anyway, I don't know how much longer I can last; if something doesn't happen soon I think I'm going to blow my brains out!

Was it an accidental overdose? An intentional overdose? No one knows, and in some ways, that question isn't important. I must forget about everything. I must repent and forgive myself and start over; I can't stop life and get off. Besides, since I've thought about my dad dying from alcohol addiction, I don't want to die. I'm afraid. Isn't that ghastly and ironic? I'm afraid to live and afraid to die.

I didn't tell anybody, but I neglected the doctor's advice as to regular visits, to stop drinking or taking coke. I just started to drink more to take more cocaine to numb the pain. I felt happy and free as a bright canary chirping through the open, endless heavens. And I was so relaxed! I simply haven't the energy or the strength or the desire without them

BTW, having sex on coke is like lightning and rainbows and springtime

I keep asking myself how I could be such an idiot! A stupid, ugly, senseless, foolish, ignorant idiot! If there were medals and prizes for stupidity and ugliness, I certainly would receive one. The only thing I am longing for now is to throw away my sleeping pills and antipsychotics, and become myself again! Or will I spend the rest of my life feeling like a walking disease?

Are There Consequences to my Actions?

Everything we do in life has a consequence and everything that is done to us has a consequence. As a child I believed many untrue things about myself, I accepted answers from unreliable sources and drew the conclusion that I wasn't good enough and I had to make people want me and love me. Prostitution was the destination I ended up in because I took a path that led me far from who I truly was.

Being as desperate as I was to fill the hole within me had its consequences. I was putting myself in danger in so many ways. Not just the danger of being caught by a cheating husbands wife or being caught by my own husband, no the danger was far greater than that.

Seeking new clients came with its own list of red flags. But for me, I did not care.The need to feel loved to be needed by someone seemed far greater than the risk of getting hurt. Even the money paid led to dangerous liaisons. I think the risks were what drew me,thrill-seeking got my adrenaline pumping. But it led to carelessness, loss of friends and relationships. Each thrill each danger led to me needing more and more to fulfil my desires, my wanton needs, this insatiable appetite for destruction.

At this point, I had three websites and two mobile phones so clients would either call me to book or message me through one of my websites. We would discuss the requirements and price and once agreed arrange to meet. I would usually drive to wherever the meeting place was(usually a hotel, but sometimes their home).

Other sexual encounters arose from late nights out in bars leading to quickies against a wall or somewhere secluded from the bright lights of the city.No payment for this was received but a free night out and as much alcohol and drugs as I wished to consume.

I always thought I was ultimately in control but I was actually putting myself in danger every time and even when things did go badly it did not dissuade me from continuing.

It was late one evening when I headed to a bar I had not been to before. I could hear music blaring from inside and this drew me in. I was cold-blooded and deliberate as I approached the bar to order a drink, aware of the eyes looking me over.

I was something to look at with my slim figure and large breasts and buttocks that just gave the right curve in any dress or jeans. On this particular night, I was wearing skintight leather trousers a corset leaving my breasts bulging over and 4-inch heels. My red hair fell onto my shoulders seductively in loose curls, my piercing blue eyes lined in dark eyeliner and lips that were irresistible. I knew everyone would look. Even the way I walked to the bar was shameless and artful.

I ordered whisky on the rocks, the bartenders eyes never leaving me as he poured a large measure. I gulped it down. "another please" I ordered to him. Again his eyes never left me as he poured another large measure and plopped to ice cubes into a glass. This time I savoured the drink, running my finger around the edge of the glass in a sensual manner. Taking an ice cube from the glass and putting it to my mouth and sucking on it for a moment before returning it to the whisky. Licking my lips seductively. "That's a good whisky I said none of that cheap shit they serve you across the road" my voice low and husky. The bartender nods in agreement his cheeks flushing scarlet red.

The guy sat next to me is moving closer to me, among others in the bar who are gravitating towards me. I humour them all for a few hours whilst they take turns to buy me the next drink. Adjusting myself on the stool to reveal my long legs, leaning towards them as they whisper into my ear so that my breasts are visible. Toying with my hair wrapping it around my fingers entwining it in my long red painted nails. I have their undivided attention, I can see their semi bulging cocks, the way they move awkwardly to adjust themselves.

"Now which one of you lovely boys wants to fuck me tonight" my voice devilish laughing out loud as I see the shocked but wanton looks in their eyes. I take one by the hand and pull them to the open space by the jukebox. It's like lambs to the slaughter. I push the coin into the slot and press b9 . The track "I touch myself" begins as I start to dance encouraging all the eager guys desperate to touch me. Soon one is behind me his hands on my waist he wants to lead me with his grinding but I take control pressing my self against him and moving rhythmically to the music. I'm surrounded each one waiting for their turn with me. I'm exquisite, thrilling to them my mind urgent and focused on a single goal.

It was getting late, only a few men remained desperately waiting for my company. I was pretty drunk by now and decided that I'd got bored of toying with them, no one was really going to whisk me away to a beautiful island where I would be happy and free.

My mind is now talking to me asking "What are you doing? don't you want to go home and curl up in your duvet," well its too late now you stupid girl, now you will have to be fucked for a few hours, you will be desperate for sleep, your body exhausted from its performance, but even as the sunrises you will be watching, waiting for them to succumb to sleep so your exit can be made, and then only then will that feeling you carry be lifted for a moment as you walk yourself home along the quiet streets of early dawn. Tears will be stinging your eyes, you will be exhausted, your feet moving of their own accord step by step until you reach your front door.

It's hard to put the key in the lock, but you turn it and open the door. The shoes that you have already removed to take the long walk home you discard in the hallway along with your Jacket and purse. The climb up the stairs to your bedroom filled with difficult thoughts. Gently you open the bedroom door, he lays there in his silent slumber unaware of the trauma you are burden with. You slip gently beneath the duvet and sleep so deep it feels as if you have fallen through the mattress.

I awake several hours later, my mouth dry with a bitter taste I know well. It's hard to move my head from the pillow the whisky leaving its mark. My body aches all over every movement brings me pain, I am lost in my shame tears falling down my face.

Events of last night are being replayed in my mind, I don't want to watch this movie, I don't want to see the truth of what happened.

I discard the duvet and lift my head, my hair is tangled, makeup smudged on my face, my body bruised. "I deserve this, I really do," I tell myself. But inside I'm crying loudly my cries suffocating me so I can hardly breathe. Reality is something I find hard to accept and this particular one would stay in my mind for a long time.

Upon leaving the bar that evening where I had spent my time teasing men until their hard pricks throbbed desperately for release it had not gone how I intended it. Three of us walked a little way through the park to one of their houses. I was still full of laughter and flirtatious banter even though my brain was telling me to stop. It was too late for that and I knew it. I would have to continue on this path and just get it over with.

187

More alcohol was offered upon arrival I sat gingerly on the sofa waiting for one of them to make a move, but they did not. Clearly, they were waiting for me. We sat and chatted and sipped our drinks, I'm unsure as to how much time passed but it felt like an eternity. Eventually, I made my move. "Do you have anything else to drink?" I asked. He replied yes and got up heading towards the kitchen, I followed watching him as he opened the fridge and took out a beer. "Here," he said handing me the bottle. I reached out to take it from his hand and fell into him. We laughed at my drunken fall and then the moment was here I kissed him squeezing his buttocks as I did so. My kiss hard and urgent enough for him to respond. The bottle of beer fell from my hand as he pushed me hard against the worktop pulling at my bustier to free my breasts. He was rough and strong kissing and groping me. I stopped for a moment and looked into his eyes, again my mind saying "why are you doing this?" But I knew the answer to that.

At this point, his friend had come to see what we were doing and upon seeing his mate kissing me decided he was going to join in. He soon had his cock out hard and throbbing, rubbing it as he watched us. I thought I had them in the palm of my hands, but oh god how wrong was i. My bustier was ripped from me and his cock forced into my mouth before I had a chance to act he was so force full I was choking, but he was relentless stopping just enough to allow me to gasp for air, the guy I had been kissing was undoing my trousers. Once he had them down far enough that he had access to my pussy he pushed my knickers aside and forced his fingers into me. I thought it best to play along to try and minimise injury but I knew I had made a mistake. Before I knew it he had my knickers in his hand ripping them off, his friend now pulling my trousers from me. I was in trouble I had teased the wrong men. "Stop !" I screamed out and with that, I was punched in the face. "shut up slut, we are going to fuck you till you beg us to stop." and they both laughed. They twisted my arms up behind my back and forced me face down onto the kitchen floor. I tried to resist but they were too strong for me. One sat on me and tied my wrists together with his belt whilst the other penetrated me. Once my wrists were secured they took it in turns to fuck me in whatever position they could one would fuck my pussy whilst the other fucked my arse at the same time. I thought I would rip in two. I mentally closed down. My body had been pushed to the limit but it didn't die. They beat me around the head and left bite marks on the inside of my legs and on my buttocks. When they had finished they released my hands. And went about like nothing had happened. I gathered my things up and got dressed in what was salvageable. I sat on the end of the settee waiting for them to fall asleep so i could leave.

I realised that men knew they could offer me money and that they could be violent towards me.

Yes, I was a prostitute who exchanged money for sexual activity but anything outside of the agreement or a failure to pay is rape. I was raped."

Forcing or coercing someone to perform sexual activity under the threat of violence or through physical force is rape. Consent can be given and then withdrawn at any point.

Strangers with benefits

Sex is something people do when they love each other deeply. At least, that's what most of us are taught as children, if we're taught *anything* about sex. But that's not always how it goes. Sometimes, you have the hottest sex with someone you don't even like. I know, because I've done it.

It's six o'clock in the morning and the clubs are now shut. Respectable citizens are up and walking their dogs. The rest of the world is sleeping. But for junkies, the party has just started.I go there and see them all with their wild eyes and I feel at home. I don't have to hide in a corner and I can ask any stranger "what you got?" and then after I've snorted a few lines they are now my closest soul mate.I enjoy my few hours of artificial happiness

Her name was Suzi and we met at a party three years ago. At first, she seemed great. She spent half the night teaching me how to play pool. But after a week of texting, I realized that we'd never work in a relationship. Our politics and values were wildly mismatched, she said things that made me cringe so hard my eyes felt like they'd pop out of my head, and she was a chronic liar. Still, we had loads of sexual chemistry and I didn't let that go to waste. We had casual sex for five months.

We had decided to meet at the Turks as this great rock band were playing that evening and listening to live music always cheered me up, but I was in such a dark place and all I wanted was to get drunk take Suzi home and fuck each other hard, no emotion no feelings just raw animal lust, but Suzi wanted more from me. She thought she could help me change my bad habits but I didn't need her help.

I stood outside the bar cigarette hanging from my lips my short skirt and knee-high boots leaving nothing to the imagination. Suzi comes outside "much happen last night?" she reverts her gaze as I look into her eyes. "Kiss me" I smile at her and she plants her soft lips on mine. Standing under the canopy of the smoking area the street light glowing on us. She puts her hand on my inner thigh and feels the marks. I grab her arm tightly and hold her "I don't know why I do this, I just need...need to feel" I whisper to her. I'm a little drunk already so my emotions are spilling over and something about her touching my hidden cuts pulls on my heartstrings.

I cry a little into her shoulder but she pushes me away angrily. I know she wants answers she stares at me. I kiss her on the forehead and the cigarette falls burning on my arm. Suzi knows there are more burns and I know she wonders why.

"Why," Suzi says

There is no answer to that Suzi stands there desperation in her face she sees how sad I am and hugs me tightly."Just please stop doing this to yourself"

I light another cigarette

"Smoking will kill you you know" her voice full of concern

191

"Fucking good" I reply cold and stoic as normal

"I don't understand you sometimes, I give you advice and you never listen.I hold you while you cry and you ignore me until your in some huge depressive state and it all washes over you and then you need me," Suzi says annoyed she's fed up with me using her.

"I don't need this right now Suzi I just want us to fuck I don't need you to sort my problems for me" I look at her with a look that could kill

"I'm not trying to care for you" she promises

"Just fuck off Suzi" I shout and push her out of my way

"You're a selfish bitch.Why don't you fuck off back to the bar and drink yourself to death" I spat back at her so angry and headed back to the bar for another drink. Suzi didn't reply and just walked off home leaving me regretting what id said. And yes I was so selfish and didn't really care about anyone but myself, it's just that's who I was back then. Constantly pushing people away when they tied to get close to me. I left with some guy from the bar in the early hours of the morning. I wanted Suzi in my bed really but he would feel the vacuum for now.

I know going home with men when I'm drunk normally ends in tears and this was just another of those occasions.

When I awoke that next morning I could not recollect the night before but was used to waking up in some random bed. I was always left with bad feelings and shame. My hair was stuck to my neck and there was vomit down my top I hurt all over my pupils were dilated and my make up streaked down my face. I pulled myself together and staggered to the bathroom picking up my knickers skirt and boots and redressing. I turned on the tap and filled the sink. Grabbing a face cloth I tided my face up. I could see in the mirror my breasts were badly bruised and there were violent love bites on my neck. I gathered my things and walked out onto the empty streets it was around 6:30 am. I began to cry knowing that the night's events had hurt me not only physically but mentally. I just kept walking until I reached Suzi's front door. Would she answer I didn't really want to see her like this but I had nowhere else to go?

Suzi opened the door dazed from sleep wrapped in her dressing gown. She looked at me and pulled me inside closing the door behind me I began to sob hardly able to communicate. Suzi walked me upstairs and I laid on her bed my crying now louder. I was in a state I felt so stupid it was ripping me apart I couldn't understand why I did this to myself.

Suzi held me stroking my hair allowing me to let it all out." I'll run a bath" she whispered. returning to the bedroom to find laced out half asleep she proceeded to remove my top pulling it up over my head. She removed my jewels and I just stared as her hands touched my bare skin. She pulled off my boots and the rest of my clothing. Placing a kiss on my forehead she held my naked body scooped me up and carried me to the bath. She was looking at me the whole time full of concern. Taking the sponge she dipped it in the soapy water and proceeded to wash the vomit from me."Oh Eva my little disaster what am I going to do with you"

I was silent but held her hand. taking a jug she washed my hair lathering it with shampoo that smelt of coconuts and I felt safe. I started to cry but it wasn't the shampoo in my eyes just a realization of the night's events.

Suzi finally finished washing my entire body so I stepped out into the warm fluffy towel she wrapped around me. I stood there whilst she dried me feeling the comfort of a child being dried by a parent. She puts in a big t-shirt and I curl up under her bedcovers. I Fall into a deep slumber.

Our friends-with-benefits situation ship ended dramatically, with Suzi sobbing into my lap begging to be with me. Since then my friends have all asked me: "Why were you having sex with her? You didn't even like her." The answer is simple: The. Sex. Was. GOOD. There's nothing as sexy as your girlfriend coming legs bent in a diamond shape the loudness of the vibrator and the timing of my stokes to the shaking of her knees. And then the zen-like whooshing of her breathing as she begins to come for the second time.

People have sex for lots of reasons. Sometimes that reason is a deep, loving connection with a partner. Sometimes that reason is stress relief, connection, or it just feels good,"

Suzi was the first person in a long time to whisper, "What do you want me to do to you?" in my ear. With her, I was able to explore positions and ~activities~ I had longed for but had not been in a position to act on...

Time moves like clockwork, only stopping when the batteries die. I believed life was sort of like that, always moving forward whether you want it to or not. But then one day unexpectedly you wither away and die, like the frozen hands on the clock face and the forgotten memories in an attic your parents never clear.

Harry however was different in the case that she never moved forward. But this wondrous girl plagued me, like a sort of chickenpox. You get over it and never have it again, but it leaves a lifelong scar.

The truth is I knew I was trying to find a replacement for Harry and Suzi wasn't it I just decided to overlook the parts I didn't like. Our connection was basically about sex, not her personality.

This went the same for all those I had sex with whether for money, pleasure, or some other kind of payment.

I had regular places I went to drink and look for possible sexual encounters that would lead to some financial benefit, or maybe just to fulfill the self-fulling prophecy I had created for myself.

I had my favourite black dress on, the backless one that clung to my figure, that made me an object of men's desire. it had its own sexual magnetism. Even my husband would go crazy when I wore it. It was like it sent electric shocks of sexual energy to those that I would pull in with such ferocious intensity. whatever it was it was beyond my control I this hot, young woman with a body that said I want to kiss your lips even though we have never even spoken so all you want to do is touch the bare skin of the gorgeous entity taking up space on the other side of the bar.

The evening would follow its usual pattern, ordering a drink at the bar, watching to see who notices me, and then finding a way to start a conversation. Once I had approached a man the rest just flowed naturally.

He was a businessman and had come to reading for that reason alone, well that and an opportunity for sex. After endless drinks and chitchat he had booked a table at his favourite Turkish restaurant, so invited me to join him. I obliged, jumping through the necessary hoops to get to my end goal of sex in exchange for a large quantity of cash. I had already ascertained that he had a large quantity of cash when he produced the large wad from his pocket to pay for my drinks. Again when he ordered whole bottles of whisky at the swanky Turkish restaurant in portabello road I knew I was on to a winner.

The atmosphere and food was amazing and this was something that I really enjoyed as over the years I had acquired a refined and passionate taste in food and culture. I knew how to behave in this refined environment , but on entering the hotel lobby later that evening I felt I stuck out like a sore thumb. The grand marble entrance was huge and echoed the high quality of the place. It was empty apart from the hotel receptionist and concierge.

He paid for the room took the key and we went up in the lift.

Ok, so now things were getting real. Yes id had a fun time, the food was amazing and everyone had enjoyed my company, but the winning and dining were over and now I had to perform.

He untied the strap of my dress from my neck so it fell away revealing my naked breasts.I let him play with them for a few minutes but time was getting on and I needed to get done and get home and now being in London at 3 am was an issue. The kids had school in the morning. I needed to do him fast.

I walked him to the edge of the bed and pushed him back. Slipped off my dress leaving me naked apart from my lacey thong.

Luckily for me, middle-aged men who have consumed large quantities of alcohol normally don't last long, are too drunk and fall asleep, or can't get it up. I'm hoping he won't take long, that having some young , sexy woman riding his cock will push him to the edge. After twenty minutes of my best ever performance, he is snoring. Thank fuck for that it's now nearly 4 am and I really do need to get home so I can function tomorrow, but he hasn't paid me!

Sod it I grab my dress and freshen myself up. His trousers

are hanging over the back of an armchair, I delve into the pocket and take the wad of cash out. I have no idea how much is there but it will have to do. He's still snoring I pick up my shoes and creep out of the room.

Once down in the lift I head to the concierge and order a taxi. "That will be 80 is that ok?" he says looking me up and down

"ok thanks "I reply politely. Yes, I know it's now so obvious to you what I am. Young women late at night, businessman twice my age, expensive hotel, only been 30 minutes now I'm leaving in a taxi. I feel instantly angry and want to shout out "yes I'm a prostitute do you have a problem with that!" but I don't I wait for the taxi to pull up and take me home. I'm silent the whole way back to my front door, I have exhausted any necessity for chit-chat with him. I hand him 80 in cash and walk to my front door.

5 am shit only two hours and the kids will be up. The house is in darkness as always and I close the front door as quietly as I can and creep upstairs to my bedroom. I open the door my husband is sleeping soundly. I discard my dress and creep under the covers relishing the warmth and nod off to sleep. Tomorrow I will be greeted with the usual questions of what time I came home, and as usual, I will lie because my husband has no idea what time I came home. The school run will be tiring but at least once dropped off I can return to my bed for a couple of extra hours of sleep and wake refreshed to be the perfect mother when I greet them at the school gates later. Only then do I look in my bag at the wad of cash. I count it out 500! I can't believe my luck but also there is an uneasy feeling that the man I was with has woken to find all his money gone and will come looking for me. I brush these feelings aside and

think about what I will spend it on. Later that day I purchase myself an electric acoustic guitar and enjoy my few hours of happiness from my purchase.

Yes, I did hear from him again but only to ask me if I got home ok!

The end of the beginning

The note of pity, the hushed tone of concern, the carefully sculpted facial expressions of anguish—I became so sick of these that, in response to strangers' questions about the contours of my family or the number of my siblings, I stopped mentioning my brother at all. It was easier on everyone to airbrush him from the record, and anyway, my brother was in prison, so what did he care if I pretended he was never born?

I loved my brother from the moment my mother brought him home. He was so tiny his little face so serene, I would hold him in my arms for hours. I begged my mother to let him sleep in my room so I could just watch him, sleeping like an angel.

Little was I to know what would grow between us over time.

After leaving my husband for the umpteenth time I had packed a bag and gone to my mothers, my head bent in shame at my lack of being able to hold down a relationship.I hated running to her but at least I was safe.

Lying in the dark in my mother's living room I tossed and

turned on the hard mattress of the pull out bed. My two boys sleeping peacefully top to tail on the sofa next to me. I wished I could drift off into a childlike sleep, but I was always disturbed by thoughts and dreams.

It was late definitely past midnight, my eyes were heavy as I started to drift off to sleep. I do not know what time it was when I became aware of another presence in the room. The blanket I had covered myself with was pulled down to my feet, my t-shirt pushed up towards my breasts. Someone was touching me, I felt their fingers brushing against the lips of my pussy.For some reason, I was too afraid to open my eyes, so I decided to pretend I was still asleep. I closed my eyes as tightly as I could as if to wipe this memory or dream from my mind, accept it was not a dream at all. The fingers were pushing more forcibly now and I wanted them to stop I wanted to not be violated. I had come here to be safe! I clenched my legs harder together hoping this would deter whoever it was that was violating me. It did not there was some hesitation that I felt, but then moments later the fingers started again, stroking me trying to push between my delicate folds. Again I held my breath and kept my eyes tightly closed fearing to see the person who was doing this to me.

Anger, confusion, and despair were building up inside me and with those feelings, I tried to grab one last attempt to be left alone. I rolled over onto my side as if in sleep startling the perpetrator who then left the room. I lay there in disbelief as to what had happened, feeling ashamed at myself for not shouting out or something, but the fear of knowing who the perpetrator was had paralyzed me. Eventually, I opened my eyes there was no one there just me and my beautiful boys sleeping soundly. I pulled down my t-shirt gathered up the blanket and wrapped myself tightly in it.

I tried not to cry, I was never going to be sacred, was I?

That night a massive stain had been made on my heart and my soul.

It was many years later that I came to know who had molested me that evening.

Being a child who had been abused from an early age and then gone onto another abusive relationship had left me feeling that maybe I was to blame. Why did all these men abuse me, was I giving them some kind of consent?

I was so confused, it must be me, surely all this abuse couldn't just happen to one person. But it did.

All these responses to my abuse are valid. Fear, anger, and rage were often the most understandable, but I loved my abusers, too. That love didn't vanish the second that abuse occurred, in fact, I relied on that love to conceal and even to let it continue. I was trying to preserve my family.

I had to remain resilient somehow. And so I kept my secret hidden deep down in the depths of my soul.

This person who I had loved from the day he was born had become another in a long line of abusers. And again I still loved him.

Later he was called out for the abuser that he was when my son aged five hit me with the devastating recollection of molestation from my brother. I had failed as a mother, I had allowed this perpetrator access to my children by hiding the shame of what he was and this enabled him to abuse my son. My world was crashing down around me I could hardly breathe as I heard the words from my innocent child's mouth. I thought I was going to lose all hope I wanted to give up to be swallowed up by all that dark matter that lived inside me.

But strangely I mustered up all those feelings into courage and rang the police and social services. Yes, I had lost my family but I had done what was necessary to protect my child. This became one of the most painful experiences that I would ever live through.

"It is like the memory is shattered glass, and over time, a few little pieces of that glass come back together, but it isn't a whole and complete memory,"

As with all things in my family they were forgotten over time hidden in the cracks that were papered over, swept under carpets, or locked away in cupboards. And so I fell back into the comfort of my hidden secrets and life resumed as normal, well as normal as could be for me.

Life continued on even if I didn't want it to. My brother went to prison and I visited him every fortnight. He grew up into a man, my children grew into teenagers, and the love I had for my brother remained.

We socialized together, our secret like some kind of bind we couldn't break. He was the same as me, we both wore the same mark. We drank took drugs and egged each other into sexual encounters. My brother took a lot of pride in finding suitable men to satisfy my urges. We felt like we were indestructible when together often talking of our special bond when alone and drunk.

He was so much more fortunate though, my mother had covered up his secrets and misdemeanors leaving my brother with an unmarked record. He went on to succeed in every venture jumping from promotion to promotion sometimes clinging to the edge but always scooped up into the arms of my mother's impenetrable shield.

It was one of these particular nights that led to that moment the one I knew was imminent somehow. My brother always touched me inappropriately and we had ended up kissing on more than one occasion this was a decision that has made most of our adult lives aimless and cloudy. I will not write about the act itself but what took place was the thing I'm most ashamed about of all the wicked and evil things I have done. Not only was it the biggest taboo of all but it was the thing that I began to crave and I knew I could never go back from here on. Our love was beautifully corrupt and had risen from two polar opposites.

He had been so loved and nurtured whilst I on the other hand had been so unloved and abandoned and somehow this had conjured up something dark in both of us. We were opposite ends of the spectrum but I discovered there was a fine line between good and evil.

Our love for each other seemed to be liberating but Lust literally means over-desire. It is when you take something that is good, twist it, and add cravings to it so you are consumed until you are gratified. It was destructive, it turned us into deceivers and manipulators was like getting some sort of fix. My brother only loved himself when we were getting physical I was just the object of his gratification.

"Lust is always ugly because it is self-indulgent and self-centeredness is never a pretty thing.

We did not speak of what happened till many years later when he was in his thirties and I was approaching forty. And when we did it changed everything.

I'm certain the naming of this terrible act with words, on paper, is a cathartic way to transform the isolated, shameful pain into beauty.

Are you by yourself in a bathroom, crying with a blade? My words are trying to find you. Your words have found me.

I understand the thought. My family and friends want to know that I'm better now, that I've found some kind of closure. I don't dispute that cathartic writing has its place—generally under lock and key in a private diary, not on a bookshelf for all to see. I would never deny pen and paper to a person in search of catharsis, but the kind of writing that spoke most deeply to me was ruthless and controlled.

Anyone who has written a book knows, there are a thousand other, easier ways to make yourself feel better, alcohol, masturbation getting a dog.

For "survivors of abuse" as we are known closure is a little more than a nice idea. This is not to deny that I had private reasons and public reasons to write a book. The private reasons came from an impulse to describe a period of my life in a language that had a ring of truth to it. To give my experiences meaning and form. It involved an impulse to transfigure the horrific events into a compelling story, in other words into a work of art.

The public reasons came from an impulse to make others accountable, or to show others who had not had my experiences a little bit of what it's like. To write a truly comprehensive account of what it's like to live in the shadow of my abuse would make a book that was brutally sad or maybe brutally boring.

I would stare at the blank screen, day after day trying to make my life come alive in a language that would make people recoil in horror.

So then what could I write?

Neither my mother, father, or siblings knew what had troubled me for years, but eventually, I had unearthed my story and it helped me understand what the thing was.

I thought about it every day for years and it made me depressed.

Making the unbearable bearable is a massive exercise in self-deception. I became so uncomfortable with my own existence and having to find ways to perpetuate the discomfort of day to day living to make me feel the comfort of uncomfortable. Because let's face it no one wants to hear about abuse. It speaks a misery beyond words.

I had imagined that writing my book would be difficult, but it was like turning on a tap and I found my fingers flying across the keyboard. I was writing my story. The story of my dysfunctional childhood and the abuse I suffered throughout my teenage years, my experiences of rape and torture, my descent into the black hole of depression.

And as I wrote I sensed a release as my experiences appeared on paper. I had thought that my years of psychotherapy would have wiped away the memories, but writing about them helped me to deal with the past. When it came to writing the most difficult and painful events I wondered if they were too painful or controversial to share.

I also knew in doing so that there would be friends and family that would never speak to me again. Maybe I should have considered the effect it would have, but I do not regret writing or publishing my book.

Ultimately I wrote my book for me.

I do not mean to offend anyone with my raw testimony. I felt

205

that I needed to shout it out to the world in order to heal one day, so get ready to feel the anxiety, the critique. I'm writing this in the midst of chaos – the chaos is my own mind.PTSD. I am writing this to make my thoughts clear to myself, and to someone else like me who feels completely alone in this.

The bravest thing i ever did was continuing my life when i wanted to die.

Pimps and punters

pimps recruit women at nightclubs, strip bars, shopping malls, schools, college campuses, and neighborhoods and streets known for prostitution, as well as via online and social media channels.

Most of the pimps have served time for pimping or trafficking at least one minor. The few who admitted to intentionally recruiting minors say they did it because younger women are easier to manipulate, work harder to earn money, and are more marketable. Pimps typically use a variety of psychological methods of manipulation to persuade girls to conduct sex work, such as flashing money around, seducing them, entering into romantic relationships, convincing them that they may as well make money if they're already having sex, or having other female employees sell the idea.

"All the years I was a prostituted woman, I was always with Steve (being pimped). They (the police and the authorities) never did him (had him arrested or charged).

"As blokes went with me (sexually), I couldn't cut off emotionally so I started to take drugs to block down the pain. I had a deep sense of shame and it was paralysing me.

"All the prostitutes I know, and I know hundreds, are actresses. They don't enjoy it. They're just doing it for the money or drugs or whatever. Any pretence of pleasure men hear from them is just to get them to finish off quickly.

Even I took a girl, who, like me, was completely fucked up and hated the world, She thought it a bit strange because we were told to sit at the bar, not talk to each other and were given lots of cocktails. . I was 15 she was 13. On that first night, the men took her to our flat and gang-raped her for 6 hours. There was a queue of men outside the door; one would finish and another would come in. I don't know how she survived or how I made it out alive.

I go by this kebab shop several times a week and we do it on the shop floor. And he always cautions me to use the client bathroom, not the employee bathroom, because one of his female employees might have an STD. Where does he think I have been all day, at the library?"

"Almost every guy thinks he's an exception and his ego doesn't want to let him pay … Younger guys are especially bad and I have had them steal back the money while I wasn't looking."

"In addition to sex, the guy wants to cuddle which, even though he has technically paid for my time, irritates the hell out of me. I am speeding my ass off and the last thing I want to do is play statue with some needy stranger. This is agony."

They all have their own thing. There was a client I used to see once a week , I thought him a bit strange the first time when he said "you're not worried that I'm going to rape you are you?" and asked me to lift my skirt so he could spank me.

I thought is that it? The second time I walked into his room he asked me to remove my knickers and lift up my skirt and to bend over whilst he wanked himself off firing his hot come over my buttocks. He never fucked me not once.

Another guy who strips me down with fake roughness puts me face-down on the bed. Restrains and gags me, not too tightly, with torn strips of sheets, ankles fastened to wrists. Luckily I'm flexible. It comes in handy.

He sits in a chair across the room, naked, jerking off, while I struggle and moan. Finis. Thirty minutes all-in, if that. A towel he puts on the floor in front of him ensures no sticky clean-up.

And then there's Double Dom that's what we call him Molly and I would do him together. He always drives down from up north about once a month and he stinks, so we always run a bath for him which he complains about every time as it's wasting precious sucking and fucking time.

We tag team him in the tub trying to clean the clingons from his arse without him noticing. He is so gross. He always smells. Getting my face close to his groin or trying to find his tiny dick among the fat rolls makes me nauseous. He's an awful lot of work. We will trade off quick breaks under a variety of pretenses, he complains every time one of us leaves the room. It takes 12 hours!. Neither of us thought he'd want a girl on his dick the entire flippin' time.

We are both exhausted!

Tony my welsh client who's in his fifties books me whenever he is in London. I guess he's married as he wears a wedding ring. he requests I come to the hotel room with just my lingerie on under my coat. Luckily it's tipping down with rain so my belted mac doesn't look too conspicuous. I put jeans on so I don't look so obvious walking into his posh hotel lobby, then I whip them off in the fancy loos.

The staff never bat an eyelid when I emerge with my coat tightly belted, in stockings and high heels. They've seen it all before.

Tony always opens the door and meets me with a massive gin. He wants to do it on the desk and quickly because he has a business dinner to attend.

By 7:30 I'm leaving the hotel with £350 cash and my jeans back on.

Then there's Edward he likes the girlfriend experience. I go to his place and he uses a sex toy on me. He never wants me to touch him and sometimes we don't even have sex just chat.I occasionally orgasm, although with nine out of ten clients I fake it.Afterward, we cuddle on the sofa and he shows me pictures of his kids. Neither of us mentions that I'm younger than his daughter.

I frequently met married couples. Half of these couples of course are fictitious so a "wife" is also a prostitute. But there are real married couples too. And they don't always need just lesbian sex with the wife, and "ordinary" sex with the husband. There are lots of variations me, his wife, and a strap-on, or me him and a strap-on. Sometimes the other half of the couple just watches.

Yes, I was a prostitute who exchanged money for sexual activity but anything outside of the agreement or a failure to pay is rape. I was raped."

Forcing or coercing someone to perform sexual activity under the threat of violence or through physical force is rape. Consent can be given and then withdrawn at any point.

I was prostituted from 13 till I was 18. I got out because

I chose to live. The guy I was with was very violent and I ended up in the hospital a lot. I remember the nurse yelling at me once for being a prostitute. She sewed me up without anesthesia and I left the hospital feeling so shamed. I was paralyzed for 3 days. Those 3 days made me think. I decided to catch a train and leave without knowing where I was going. I stayed for 2 years after that, but that was the beginning of my exit.

I could hear what was happening to other girls and would think, at least what's happening to me isn't as bad. You have to survive. If I saw someone else looking scared, I'd think at least that's not me. It's hard for me to live with the fact that I know some women disappeared—I feel guilty.

One punter actually resuscitated me and then carried on doing what he was doing to me. I was getting to the point where I wanted to kill the punters or myself.

I would see injuries on me after punters had used me and not know where they'd come from. I mentally closed down. My body had been pushed to the limit but it didn't die. At the time I thought I was choosing punters, but now I realize that men knew they could offer me money and that they could be violent towards me

Punters are so arrogant. If you're going to be a bastard, it's easier to stick to prostitutes because no one really listens to or believes prostitutes. One reason men are angry with prostitutes is that they can't destroy them. Most men don't want to use condoms- they don't come to prostitutes for that. If someone had given me a condom I wouldn't have had the self-esteem to use one. I didn't feel like I deserved to live or not get a disease. I look back at the escorting and think those punters really hated me.

My first time I suppose were all the times his friends had sex with me in his flat whilst I was drunk or half drugged. But the first real client for me was easy like I had been doing it all my life.

I thought to myself was that it? However it turned out very differently, it was incredibly difficult to live like this, and much more difficult to get out of.

Sex becomes not the desire of two soulmates, flying in the sky and enjoying it, but a physical process. In the beginning, I occasionally would enjoy it with a good-looking man and sometimes had an orgasm, but later it disappeared. I felt more and more disgusted, and so I had sex like I was on autopilot I would be thinking do we have milk at home? or shit I need to pick up my dress from the dry cleaners.

Outside of work, I enjoyed sex with Steve and Harriet but this too was starting to fade.

So for the myths. I can read and write and I do know that the earth is round.

Not all prostitutes have their IDs taken away and are chained to a radiator by a pimp. It was like that in the nineties but not now.

Prostitutes hardly have any free time, on average I would have 4-5 clients daily each punter demands approximately 30 minutes.

A prostitute is not a nymph who likes sex so much that she decided to earn money from it.

There are no x- prostitutes

You probably will never identify a good-looking prostitute, otherwise, she will tell you. We are among you!LOL

The restoration was a long road of learning to trust, learning to love and be loved, and Learning boundaries physically and emotionally. I have learned that there are good trustworthy men, and those men have earned my respect. I have learned to live without shame and to help others to let go of shame too. Without the abuse and violation of the past, I have found the beauty in life again.

I have discovered who I am and that it is ok to be me.

I am loved, I am valuable, I am worth more than money can buy and so are you.

Truth

We both know the truth i can't tell I can't forget
  She won't let me
  I remember when I least expect it Sometimes when I close
my eyes your there I'm just a scared little girl
  What you did was wrong
  I said no I didn't want to
  You took what you wanted
  Saying no wasn't enough
  I wasn't yours to take
  You said you loved me
  You do not understand
  the fluids coursing through this body are tainted by oil
  the weakest spark could set
  these hazardous bones ablaze
  devouring my frame until I return to the dust from which I
came
  and always carry a match

Truth

I tremble when his darkness
sweeps over me,
the strong allure of the unknown
pulls me in his direction
seduced by the sweet scent of destruction I lose myself in
his arms
I give myself to the night
But the pain stays the tears are still there, I know I'm
probably a distant memory to you now, but what you did
can never be undone. We both know the truth.
I lost the ability to say no and have any control over my body.
I can't ever get that back
You still have power and control over me
But I am strong, I can endure even if I can't forget.
When I'm alone things replay in my mind like a movie it's
like constantly reliving the trauma
I want there to be hope to know that nothing is unforgivable
or irreversible
When you could not break my bones you broke my soul
When your words no longer hurt me your violence did When
my body was tired the fire in you enraged When my mind was
empty your hatred filled it
When my mouth screamed you broke it with your fists When
my body was closed you forced it to open
When I ran you dragged me back
When I cried in anguish you put me in the dark
When the blood spilled you saw my pain and you watched
When i needed you you took the life from me
When I loved you you humiliated me
What we created you destroyed
What I gave you you sold

215

What I cost was my innocence
When I slept you woke me
When I looked it was not me
what you saw you created
When I wept you laughed
When I shouted you restrained me
When I had freedom you enslaved me

But I did break free and I had a life one I thought would take all the bad in me away, but it didn't I was tormented even now twenty-six years on he had scared me beyond repair. Every path I took led me back to him, every dream and ambition crushed by my uncontrollable desire for the bad in me for that dark place where that girl lived. The place in the deepest depths of my soul.

I had to break free or chose death, my desire to save myself compelled me and lead me to a new beginning, or was it the end.

Despair

Despair Hits My Heart

"I have been coming back into life – I know this is good. But this post is about my confusion, my grief, and my despair that I still do not understand what it is to be alive – beyond being a role.

I will write in the back parts of my mind, I will try to drag out the stuff that scares me, that blocks me, that still makes me wonder if I am still nothing but an object finding how to please others.

I don't know how to be human, that is not some philosophical statement, not said for pity or sympathy – it is said because the sex trade made me into a sub-human, into nothing but consumable goods.

I can copy humans and find how to fit in with humans – but underneath, hidden from view, is a deep emptiness.

I am like a machine waiting for instructions, I am off when alone – when not working or talking.

I need an audience to end my deadness.

I am learning I do not have to please.

Have to please to stay safe.

Have to please to avoid danger.

Have to please to be seen.

Have to please to stay invisible.

Have to please by speaking to their language.

Have to please by inventing truths about myself.

The role of the prostitute is to please without thought, to please without emotions, to please without knowing a past, to please without having pain.

The prostitute is never real as a human, she can never have the right to feel, to have dreams, to know a past or have a future.

The things that make a human a human are stolen from the prostituted.

How do I survive without a despair that seems to never end?

How can you remain human when you are sexually tortured so many times it is your routine?

How do you remain human when every women-hating word, concepts, and ideals are placed under your skin until you lose what or who you are?

I was whore, I was slut, I was cunt, I was a manipulator of men, I was happy hooker, I was pretend girlfriend, I was escort, I was bitch, I was preventing real rapes to real women, I was lover of degradation, I was made with no pain threshold, I had a heart of gold, I do anything for money, I could be killed coz I was nothing alive.

I was made all that and more – but I was never allowed to be human.

I cry beyond despair as the language about the prostituted in nearly every context keeps the prostituted as sub-humans.

But to become truly human, I know many that have left have to face and know the depths of what they were made – more than what was done to them – what they made by society and the sex trade taking away their access to their own humanity.

Of course, we were made dead by the thousands of rapes, batterings, sexual torturing, and closeness of a violent death.

But what made us dead, was the constant reminders it was more than the sex trade destroying us – it was being surrounded by too much of society not caring what happens to the prostituted.

Society must know and face the fact that we live with the knowledge that to be prostituted is to be nothing in life and thrown away in death.

We live in a world that would avoid prostitution unless it's thrown into their faces – and then make excuses for its existence.

Excuses excuses.

Maybe I'm already dead?

Still, call me strange, but I happen to find a certain appeal in the conviction that one is, though otherwise lucid, nevertheless already dead. Provided there were no uncomfortable symptoms of rigor mortis cramping up my hands, nor delusory devils biting at my feet, how liberating it would be to be able to write like a dead man and without that hesitating fear of being unblinkingly honest. Knowing that upon writing this I would be tucked safely away in my coffin, I could finally say what's on my mind. Of course, living life as though it were a suicide note incarnate is an altogether different thing from the crushing, unbearable weight of an actual suicidal mind dangerously tempted by the promise of permanent quiescence.

Most of my suicide attempts are driven by a flash flood

of strong emotions like wanting to escape from myself. My mind is intolerable and relentless and trying to keep me from completing the act is futile like asking me when at the peak of sexual excitement to refrain from orgasm.

I am in a constant state of suicidal ideation, my mind filled with constant vivid,affect-laden images of the suicide and aftermath of my death.

I am in emotionless vacuum thoughts turning into auditory hallucinations like some evil twin from a parallel universe. They are my rational mind and will remain locked in a tower, looking down on the soulless shell of my body, acting and reacting.

It's like fate that I will eventually kill myself, once I've unburdened myself from the torturous life I live. You see it's an aspiration not that I want it but like it's looming there in my to-do list and it hasn't been checked off yet.

I hope it will relieve the pressure of an extended existence as a cast-off.

You see if I truly unburdened myself I will have no choice but to take this course as my words once said will cause a wave of catastrophic consequences for everyone who's ever known me, and in true cowardice, I will not want to be around to face this.I simply cannot survive the realization of the devastation I will cause and the flame that was once lit inside me will have burned out at last and I will finally be free from it.

Selfish yes that I am and my selfishness should have ended long before, before that child was born, before love and marriage, before the many more babies I bore. It should have been stamped out before my infection infected others, and so now my curse lives on spreading like the virus that it is and the only cure is the frightening truth.

Despair

And now I will take a moment before I speak it

Letting go

I've spent most of my 45 years of life being angry at the world. And why wouldn't I be? Anyone who came from where I came from would be too. Not to mention that statistically, I should be dead or in jail. It's mindboggling that a momentary decision can determine so much of your path in life. I sought refuge from myself more often than not, drinking and smoking myself numb. I rather enjoyed the nothingness that came from it, anything to not feel the torment. And that worked until it didn't, and when it stopped, I understood that I would have to deal with some shit

What does it mean to let go? To forgive? I've read those words, I've heard those words, and I've written those words, but to what avail. What do they mean? I struggle to this day with the concept of forgiveness. People often say it's for you, but I would argue that it's for those that earn it. That, however, is another conversation altogether. What sticks with me the most through all the self-education, personal growth, and trauma healing is that if I was going to live my life on my terms that I was going to have to release the grip that I had on my trauma. As much as I was a part of it, it was a part of me. Everything I knew in life was childhood trauma, was abuse, but I understood that eventually, to move forward, I would have to let it go.

To be frank, I don't know that I will ever forgive some of the people that hurt me; how does one forgive their abuser I'm not there, and honestly, I likely never will be, and that is my choice. Some say that you must forgive to heal, I don't entirely agree, but then again, none of this trauma healing we put ourselves through is universal. I do know this; I no longer carry the weight of the experiences of my past. I've made a declaration that I don't have to forgive, but I do have to release what I am holding. I have repeated those words to myself a thousand times, trying to define what they mean and how to allow them to hold space in my life. What I've come to understand is that letting go means letting go, and it's either all in or all out.

And so I stare out the window the heavy rain lashing down on its pane and I realise that all the pain, suffering, abuse, torment, and healing is me. I understand it, and maybe I have accepted it and in this very moment, as tears stream down my eyes, I feel that I have finally done it. I've let go.

As I sit looking out onto the world around me, I finally get it. Letting go is about acknowledging that something terrible has happened to you, accepting that you can't change the past, choosing to release the grip that you have around it, and making a decision to move forward on your terms. And i know that there will be moments when I have to remind myself that I've let go. I carry the scars of abuse on my body and my soul. However, when I feel the anger, frustration, or sadness of my past, I will take a look out the window and remind myself that

223

I am living for me, not for them.

Memoirs

The river of memories had quieted. The memoir was clarifying into a portrait of a girl becoming a woman, caught between adoring and breaking free of her brilliant, destructive lover. As I clarified and deepened my voice, I continued to heal. And I had so much more work to do, to understand and write the whole story, as best I could

"Abuse isn't my story. Abuse is the story of those that abused me. How I live with post-traumatic stress, as well as how I parent and pay my bills and love, that's MY story." I reject the notion that sexual abuse is "my story." It's not.

I am clear on is this:

Sexual abuse is the story of the person who perpetrates violence and not the story of the person they violated.

Knowing I am a survivor of childhood sexual abuse tells you nothing about my life, my personality, or me. It tells you what I lived through.

How the trauma of sexual abuse impacts me as an adult and it impacted me as a child.

It doesn't now nor did it ever define me though. I honestly did not realize this until recently.

And I still live with post-traumatic stress. But that reality takes up far more of my air and brain than does the details of my abuse.

I decided to write.

The stories poured out, including ones I'd never told anyone. Maybe scarier than writing about the bad things that happened with my father and my abuser was to write about how I'd loved them. I had adored them both more than anyone in my childhood. It was painful to return to the heartbreak of loving and hating them, and the decades of breaking away. I had felt free of my father the day he died. I was afraid I might be seduced again by his world of whisky, and his addiction. I was afraid of getting caught in the old pain.

My father was a drunk and a sex addict who had harmed me physically and emotionally. He was also charismatic and a brilliant storyteller. He was my father who loved, abused, and trained me through intellectual seduction, grooming my mind.

He was brilliant and had an ambulant enthusiasm that attracted people to him, including me. He was fundamentally a good person, who had been knocked off balance after his golfing career ended. This doesn't excuse his behavior but makes me compassionate and understanding. He used his own pain to wound me.

Hi, abuse led me into the arms of another abuser a predator, who broke me down until I was dependant on him for the very air itself that I breathed.

It's my life I'm living – not the past. Of course, the past impacts the present. A lot. And abuse is one of the causes of

226

my post-traumatic stress. But it's not the only important part of my story. And it sure a shell is not the entirety of it.

Now as an adult I get to decide when and what to discuss, detail, or write about, either in therapy in my diary or in conversation. Totally my choice always!

I say I'm the author of my story because for so long that wasn't clear or obvious to me. I was a character in the play of my life and I didn't get to write my own lines or choose the characters or settings I lived in. That's what it is to be a child.

But I'm not a child now and abuse is not my story.

Survival is my story. Creativity is my story. Parenting is my point. Love and hope and opportunities are my priorities.

There are still some days of nightmare hangovers and being post-traumatically stressed. And there are days when I'm in bliss and a friend to another holding hope as well. Sometimes both on the same day. Often both.

But my ultimate life goal is boring and simple, to feel and ingest the experiences of my ordinary life. To parent. Walk the dog. Pet the cat. Hug. Hold hands. Plant something. Share a meal.

There's a saying, "You can't say yes until you can say no." I love that. It never felt like an option whilst I felt there was a ticking bomb in my bones.

The writing was one of the ways I used to help restore balance. But it's just one path, not THE path.

Saying, "Not here, not now, and maybe not ever with you" feels great.

Sharing in more detail than I want or if it's early or I'm stressed or I don't feel safe or the response is lousy usually makes me feel uneasy and unsettled for minutes to hours to days.

I don't have to go through that if I don't want to.

Neither do you.

Well, here's what I would say to my family if they demanded an explanation: You made this dreadful story mine. You started writing it, but now I'm going to finish it — because it is mine.

I'm reclaiming the rights to it. I can tell the story. Do what I please with it. I own it. All of its decrepit, debauchery, and encumbering, sad delirium. All of its hope, love, and choices. I choose to take it and push it out of me.

Can you understand? Are you by yourself in a bathroom crying with a blade? Are you hiding in the girls' bathroom at school? Are you wasted at the bar at 3:00? My words are trying to find you.

My plan is to continue writing and helping others.

Re-birth

As a woman now in my mid forty's I'm tortured by the life choices I have made and spend my days dreaming of the life I could have had. I toy with all kinds of ideas of what that may be but sadly none of it seems to fit and so I'm destined to remain in this life that I have created for myself. I cannot escape the ever-growing longing that I feel and have little or no understanding of what life or living actually is. Time is running out.

That was my final therapy session finished and it had been the longest fifty minutes of my life. After months of pain, I had finally left the past behind for good. I felt lighter, happier even than id ever felt before and I knew I was ready to take the next step.

It was only a short drive home, the roads were quiet the sun was out so I turned up the volume on the car stereo. I pulled up outside my house took a deep breath and walked to the front door. Luckily there was no-one home so I sat at the dining table staring at the blank page of the notepad. then I started to write.

My darling Richard

I really cannot go on. If time travel existed I would choose not to be born.

When it gets to a point where the bad outweighs the good you know it is time.

It's time to set the record straight I am the fuel of my own self-destruction. although I have at many times been the victim I have now consumed all that pain and suffering and have emerged as the perpetrator. I have inflicted the same amount of pain and hurt to those I love and surround me. I am out of control like a tornado of pain and grief. my feelings have no end or beginning I have literally taken myself apart piece by piece. the outer shell that is so bruised and battered has cracked away leaving the core exposed like a nuclear reactor I'm infecting everything that touches me. I prayed for some resolution some forgiveness but it never came. when I looked inside myself I saw a monster.I thought it was the abused child inside me but it was not, even she had been destroyed. it's best that I am contained for good before my disease infects another generation. may my family be healed by my death and not grieved.

I signed my name and place the letter in an envelope and wrote Richard on the front. I took one last look around my beautiful home then headed out the front door and started walking.

Anyone can be me

I've known a lot of bad men. Some I have written about others not.

This book isn't just about child exploitation but about my life, from a dysfunctional and abusive childhood to the person I am now.

I want people to know that you can always change your direction in life, no matter how difficult that may seem.

It takes determination, you just need to decide what you want to do and go and get it.

In reading my book you may feel that my mother was a bad mother, you may even think I was a bad mother and maybe we both were.

I'd like to say to my children that they gave me the strength to be who I am today.

I'm not dead or drugged up in some alleyway.

I have shown you all love real love. I didn't know what love was . Love and sex are not the same thing, neither are love and possessiveness. With Joshua, Matthew,adam, and Bethany love were unconditional, no matter what I did, said, or how I acted. I regret a lot of the things I have done, but they have never judged me or said that they weren't raised properly.

I am so proud to be their mother.

If you have worked in the sex industry, men think you really enjoy sex. This couldn't be further from the truth. Although I have been a sex worker for a lot of my life I was never really any good at it. The only time I felt the earth move was with Steve, Harriet, and my husband.

The point I'm trying to make is to not stereotype and to see the real person behind that deceptive deceiver.

I'd like this book to be an inspiration to women who have lost their way in the world.

I think my story is one where faith triumphs, in the end, I mean a faith where hope springs eternal and wins over insurmountable odds.

There is a shatter of light in the darkness.

Anyone can be me.

Printed in Great Britain
by Amazon